Nest of White Crows is a cross between a fast-paced whodunnit and a deep dive into the nature of racism today: Ayn Rand meets Representative John Lewis. In *Nest of White Crows*, June Gillam offers readers an inside look into the experience of well-designed racial awareness teaching, while taking us through twists and turns that make this book impossible to put down.

Christine Sleeter, author and activist,
https://www.christinesleeter.org

NEST OF WHITE CROWS

JUNE GILLAM

Gorilla
Girl Ink

ISBN/Print: 978-1-7324642-6-1

ISBN/eBook: 978-1-7324642-5-4

Cover Designer: **Karen Phillips**, Phillipscovers.com

Interior Design and Formatting: **Tarra Thomas Indie Publishing Services** tarrathomas.wordpress.com

For my sister, Janet Skalisky Dean, and brother-in-law, Alton Dean, Jr., without whom I may never have learned so much about my unconscious bias. I continue following the advice of Maya Angelou: **"Do the best you can until you know better. Then, when you know better, do better."**

PART I

CLEARWATER, CALIFORNIA, HALFWAY BETWEEN
SACRAMENTO AND STOCKTON, ON HIGHWAY 99

*We are one people with one family. We all live in
the same house ... and through books, through
information, we must find a way to say to people
that we must lay down the burden of hate. For
hate is too heavy a burden to bear.*

—The Honorable John Lewis

SUNDAY, AUGUST 15, 2021

Nothing on this hot August Sunday suggested trouble in the orchard. It was opening day at Apple Acres, and Hillary craved the simple pleasure of strolling alongside rows of leafed-out trees and picking Red Delicious.

The meteorologists predicted today's weather to hit over a hundred. Still, the cinnamon fragrance of hot apple pie à la mode had set many a mouth to watering. Hillary stepped up onto the wooden platform and guided her small group to a window to place their orders. Folk music from inside poured over the outdoor eating area while they watched for a free table.

Once seated, her teenaged daughter, Claire, and best friend, Keisha, began scarfing down their pie in a hurry as the ice cream started pooling into a milky sauce. Keisha's grandmother, Stacy, was blowing on her coffee. Hillary's yellow lab was panting from the heat.

She tipped water into the dog's travel bowl, then took a long swig from her green squeeze bottle. No pie for her. Tracking calories on her Apple Watch was her latest tactic in trying to get back under 180 pounds.

Leaving them to finish up, Hillary went inside the shop, where a fiddler was scratching out "Down in the Valley." She hummed along with the tune, one of her favorites, and waited in line to buy a frozen apple pie to take home and sturdy paper bags with handles. The price was set by the size of the bags purchased, assuming they would be filled to the top with apples.

Outside, Claire opened her bag. "This is so big! Too bad Dad had to work. He could carry more than I can."

"You plenty strong, Champ," teased Keisha, landing a soft punch on Claire's arm. Hillary smiled at the girls, who had become like sisters since they met at basketball camp a few years ago. They had their hopes set on becoming professional players, Keisha at six foot, two inches, a talented basketball center, and her own Claire, a point guard who'd inched up to five-foot-four.

The girls danced around Hillary and Stacy as if practicing their dribbling. Darius tugged at his leash, eager to run free. Hillary decided to keep the frozen apple pie with her rather than walk back to the parked car. They took off on the orchard's gravel road toward the section set aside for U-Pick.

As they passed a rotund, balding man, Hillary was startled to hear him say to his teens, "Them redskins never had it this good, stuck with bitter acorns, they was." *Redskins*. Another offensive epithet to add to her list in preparation for the ethnic studies class.

She gestured for her group to turn in at the sign marked RED DELICIOUS, ROW G. A dirt pathway ran between two rows of trees, boughs heavy with fruit crowded among canopies of oval leaves.

The rows looked like they carried on forever. Hillary paused in the sunlight and took a deep breath, inhaling the dusty, sweet scent of the place. This was a good way to spend the day.

In front of them, a scrawny woman had stopped and was pointing to a tree. "Just love these apples! Can't handle picking peaches anymore, since that Juan Corona story." Her high, thin voice carried like a piccolo in the hot air.

"Didn't he die a couple years back?" A stooped man Hillary assumed was the woman's husband stood staring at the tree. "Messed up peach trees?"

"That's what I mean, dear. You remember, in the seventies, he murdered all those poor farm workers and buried them in the orchard, went to prison for the rest of his miserable life."

Keisha led the way around the elderly couple. "Let's get past people taking the low-hanging fruit," she said.

Hillary spotted a drip irrigation pipe running along the base of the trees. "Stay in the middle if you can, reach for apples from the path," she said. "The dirt over on the sides might be muddy."

Claire sped light-footed ahead of Keisha down the long path between the apple trees. Hillary lost sight of the girls, but she knew they would return sooner or later with their bags filled. If Ed hadn't had to manage security near Sacramento's down-town arena, he'd have been here, picking apples at a fast clip. Hillary felt lucky to be married to Ed, such a good team player.

She had engaged one of Ed's friends, working as a private detective, to help look for Keisha's mother, missing since Keisha was just a year old. Hillary had confidence in him because a couple of years ago, he'd helped locate Hillary's own mother, who'd abandoned her when she was ten.

Hillary and Stacy sauntered along in the heat, sun hats covering their heads, the ties of Stacy's purple head wrap dangling alongside her neck. Hillary juggled the pie in one hand and Darius's leash in the other, trying to control the dog while he snuffled back and forth in the dirt.

The warmth of the afternoon drained the tension from Hillary's body, in high gear getting ready for the start of the fall semester. She was intent on making a success of the new class.

But today, it was time to relax, take it easy. Stacy slowed down, stepped over a shallow ditch, and moved toward a tree. "I'm going to lean against this fellow." She scuffed her foot over a low patch of ground. "This looks funny here. See? It's kind of caved in."

Darius pulled in Stacy's direction, and Hillary followed to where her friend stood. The dog started to whine and paw at the ground. "I don't want him messing with any of these irrigation pipes," she said. With a quick flip, she wrapped the leather leash twice around her wrist and tried to tug him away. "Come on, boy. Leave it."

The dog worked at the dirt. Hillary yanked on the leash. "What's come over him? He must think a bone is buried out here." As the dog dug deeper, the earth got darker and damper. He bit at something. Hillary squinted at what looked like a rope buried in the soil.

She bent to take a closer look and lost control of the pie. The box fell, its lid flying open, the pie sliding out, its domed crust crumbling. A few frozen apple slices stuck together in chunks and fell onto the soil.

Hillary ignored the pie and struggled to take the

rope from Darius, but he held it clenched in his teeth, growling softly and shaking it back and forth. Suddenly, his head snapped back as the rope broke loose and dangled from his jaws. He flung the piece of rope to the side and dug into where it had come from.

"What's he found?" whispered Stacy, wide-eyed.

Hillary studied the half-rotted fiber lying on the dirt, her stomach starting to knot up.

Something was twisted around the rope. She narrowed her eyes and peered at it. Was that a tiny piece of chain, clogged with dirt?

Just then, Claire and Keisha came back down the road, lugging bags heavy with apples, shouting out their return.

"What's our big boy doing?" Claire yelled as she ran near.

Keisha stood motionless, staring at the ground, her bag falling open, apples rolling into the shallow ditch.

"Stay back," Hillary said. "Let's go notify Apple Acres. Darius has dug up something in the orchard that needs to be investigated."

2

SUNDAY EVENING

The air hung heavy with the scent of green walnut husks starting to break open. In nearby trees, crows roosted, gathering strength to hunt tomorrow for rare fallen nuts with split shells. While the Delta Breeze pushed the day's heat off the valley floor, Professor Nettie Kovar sat on a log bench near the barn in her gnarly old orchard and addressed her students. She announced she'd just been granted tenure at Clearwater College and flashed her bright smile before she launched into the serious business of the evening.

Nettie was dead set against the college's following California's new ethnic studies law for the state universities, and she laid out the dangers ahead: group think and sloppy, emotional choices. Orientation Day would kick off Clearwater's fall semester with its mandatory ethnic studies class for first-year students, which Nettie viewed as forcing socialist drivel down student throats.

Starting their second year in Nettie's program, these young people were perched on logs circled around the empty fire pit, with no need for heat in this drought-crazed summer. In unison, they nodded as Nettie warned that incoming first-year students could be diverted by half truths preached in an ethnic studies class, lured away from the American Dream she was preparing them to achieve.

Nettie stood and swiped her dark bangs across her forehead and off to the side, emphasizing the importance of what she was about to say. "Independence. The glory of the individual, intent on fulfilling his potential!" This was what Nettie intended for these dozen students, who were earning their board and room in her White Crows program, picking the early apple crop and tending to the burgeoning walnuts in her 200-acre estate.

**

A few feet away on an incline near the fire pit, sat the bearded Army veteran Fury Underwood, a student Nettie trusted to supervise the others. Fury surveyed the tree-clogged acres. Even after working the orchard all day, an ever-present pent-up energy in his arms ached for something more to do.

With a sympathetic ear, Fury heard Nettie detail the pitfalls of ethnic studies and explain her plans to counter the threat. Over the past year, he had come to idolize the petite and charming woman, so different from his sluggish mother, now dead and buried. He was eager to support Professor Kovar's goals and to become a fellow owner of orchards one day. Her bright tones were soothing in contrast to the raspy voice of his father. Fury narrowed his eyes and thought back to those early years following the harvest, with his father supervising the farm workers.

Fury had learned to read at his father's side, from the stash of comic books stored like treasure in the humpbacked trunk of his '37 Plymouth. As a boy, he'd been proud to be nicknamed after his father's favorite character, the heroic Nick Fury.

But that was before Marvel Comics caved in and changed Nick to a Black man.

With his fists clenched, Fury watched Nettie. She flung open her hands, insisting that ethnic studies forced students to give up their individual selves, placed them into groups they had not chosen. It melted people into ethnicities, made them only Black. Asian. Hispanic. Native. Nettie's blue eyes glinted as she spoke. "Those courses want to rob you from being your unique selves. Take Lorena and

Robert, for example." She smiled at the two of them, sitting side by side. "They are individuals."

Fury opened his fists, staring imaginary holes into his palms. Why was Lorena sitting so close to that Robert Eaglefeather? And she kept going to that club on campus with that strange leader. What was her name? Something foreign, maybe from India, getting students to walk in each other's shoes or crap like that. Neka. That was her name. Neka Jay.

He rubbed his hands over his face. Damned if he would ever identify with being a Black man for anyone's sake. Not like what happened to Nick Fury in the Marvel Comics Universe. No. It was Fury's job to keep the world safe from threats, like his father had done.

Why the fuck not offer a White Studies class? Preserve the race. Lorena would fit in there with him just fine. Spanish was white, too.

He stared into the gloom of the trees and remembered the nights he'd watched his father standing proud and tall in an orchard, shovel in hand, rope set aside.

Fury reached and grabbed the shovel leaning against the barn wall. He drove it deep into the dirt. Nettie was right. Ethnic studies had to be stopped. Get back to teaching the basics.

An idea shot through his head. Over the past year, Nettie had introduced her students to her library at the big house. Fury had thumbed through her late husband's stacks of *National Geographic*. A page came to mind, the story of that Indian with the weird name. Mohandas. Come to find out, Gandhi had dropped out of school when he was young. Clearwater College would be better off without that Neka woman and others in her club.

Fury zipped up his black jacket and took a deep breath, tightening the leather across his chest. He clenched and unclenched his fists. He would wait until Nettie finished her pep talk and released the students from the log benches. She would go back to the big house and leave them here in the barn dorm.

Nettie didn't need to know what he was doing every minute. He was only helping her. He would take that loner kid Barney aside, and get him on board to set up and deliver a message on Orientation Day. Not hurt anyone. Just offer the college some good advice.

3

TUESDAY MORNING, AUGUST 17

In the dark, Hillary snuggled up to her husband's slim and sleeping body. She lay dozing, this last day before the semester started for real.

Faint musical notes from her iPhone worked their way into her dream and she woke as bouncing red apples faded away.

"What?" called out Ed, bolting upright, "I'm up!"

She waited for the familiar sound of his stumbling for the switch, then the room flooded with light.

"Too damn early," he grumbled. Hillary could hear the coffeemaker at work in the kitchen, its timer so reliable. They were up at 4:00 a.m., so Ed could leave for the airport and his flight to Mississippi.

She got up and poured them each a mug of French Roast, the coffee she was addicted to. Ed could take it or leave it but went along with her favorite. "Remind me what this conference is all about," she said as he came into the kitchen and set his backpack down,

Ed poured some of his hot coffee back into the pot and replaced it with cold water from the sink. He took a big gulp before he said, "It's the organizational behavior conference, for grads of security programs from all over. Showcasing ways to get into the heads of bad guys before they do their damage. It's in Mississippi 'cause they have such a strong MBA in the field." He drained his coffee.

"Bad guys." Hillary shook her head. "That section of the orchard where Darius dug up the rope will be excavated today. The owners were horrified at the possibility of a murder victim there. They are going through their employee records looking for bad apples, no pun intended, they said."

Ed gave his crooked smile. "It's a good thing Stacy filed that Missing Person report right away when Tamika never returned. Even back in '06 they knew to take a DNA sample from Stacy, keep it on file in case."

Hillary heaved a sigh. "It's just too far-fetched to think it could be Tamika. But that tiny chain scrap..." She rubbed her neck. "Stacy said most pictures of Tamika show her wearing a gold chain, you know?

And Keisha nearly passed out when she saw that grimy piece of chain on the ground."

Ed nodded and stood. "We'll know more after they get the excavation done." He leaned down to kiss her.

She turned to meet him full on the lips for a passionate kiss. "I'm going to miss you!" she said, surprising herself with a tear dropping onto her cheek. "Tomorrow is the first day presenting about that new class, and I'm nervous."

He wrapped his arms around her and held her tight, stroking her long hair. "It's going to be all right. You are perfect for this job. You will make a difference. I have faith in you, Chickadee."

She let herself go limp and pressed against him for a few moments. There it was. His nickname for her. She would have to talk to him about it, but some other time. He was her rock, her foundation for the jobs she'd held over the past sixteen years—reporter, journalism instructor, ghostwriter, public relations director. Now, to be co-teaching Intro to Ethnic Studies, the sound of it made her feel like an imposter. How had she ever said yes to President Williams?

"Take good care of our baby," he said as he picked up his carry-on backpack. He smirked at the look Hillary gave him. "I know, I know. Claire's a young woman now, but she'll always be my baby, too."

Hillary nodded, feeling warm all over. That was one good choice she had made in her life—marrying this man.

"Check in with Stacy, see how she's coping. And don't let your mother drive you crazy, either. Keep her out in the cottage, painting away." Hillary nodded, getting that edgy feeling as if she'd just sucked a lemon whenever her mother was mentioned.

After Ed left, she thought about going back to sleep but stayed up to work on PowerPoint slides for the class. On her laptop calendar, she could see that tonight's WNBA game would be between the Minnesota Lynx and the Connecticut Sun.

The Sun. It reminded her of why she'd accepted this job offered to her last year. Booker Williams had just been hired as president of Clearwater College. He'd served with her on the Diversity Programs Board for Sacramento's Community Center, and they'd grown to admire each other. Booker had a vision of making an Introduction to Ethnic Studies class mandatory at the college. He wanted the small private school to stay competitive with the giant CSU system, now legally bound to make students pass an Ethnic Studies class before they could graduate.

Booker had asked Hillary to co-teach the class, with their friend, Grover Zale.

At Williams's invitation, Hillary took time to

reflect on what she cared about. How to make this a fairer world for everyone. She felt it would be better for a class like that to be taught by those who had suffered more harm than she had, who had been there and experienced the pain. She decided she would say "no" to Williams' offer.

But that was just before that basketball game Hillary, Ed and Claire were watching on the TV in the basement. It was the Connecticut Sun vs the Minnesota Lynx, that day a year ago.

At halftime, a documentary ran about the women athletes and their lives off the court. Two of the Sun's players turned out to be married to each other. That was when Claire spoke up and said, "They are brave." Claire was scratching Darius's head, nuzzling him while she talked. "I feel like them, you know?" She shot a glance at Hillary.

Hillary recalled just sitting, not moving a muscle, not wanting to look at Ed.

"Darius would still love me, wouldn't you, boy?" Claire planted her face on top of his head and lifted his blond ears to press against her cheeks.

It was not something Hillary'd expected, but she stood and embraced Claire at the same time as Ed wrapped his arms around them. In an awkward group hug, they circle-danced in front of the TV, laughing and calling out, "Go, Sun!"

The Sun went on to win that day, the day Hillary faced the fact that she had so much to learn, that teaching Intro to Ethnic Studies could stretch her in ways she would never expect. She needed to understand so much more now, to support her daughter within the LGBTQ community.

The next day, she called Booker and told him she'd be honored to accept his invitation to co-teach Intro to Ethnic Studies.

For Claire's thirteenth birthday, Hillary had taken her to Mitchell's tattoo parlor. Claire selected a tiny Monarch butterfly that topped an orange-and-tan basketball, the trademarked WNBA ball, for her shoulder. Hillary got a blue swallowtail butterfly on her ankle, for the transformation she hoped would lie ahead.

In the year since then, Hillary had worked diligently to be the kind of mother Claire needed, at the same time she worked alongside Grove Zale preparing the new class. The readings and discussions were lengthy and intense. Hillary realized it would be useful if she admitted to some of her own mistakes. Or even learned how to better recognize them. At times, she felt herself floundering and began taking Darius down to run in the salt-air, leash-free section of Ocean Beach in San Francisco whenever the stress became too much. She would sit on a sand dune and gaze at the ceaseless breakers and feel her place, so small in the vast scheme of things. As small as the grains of sand she rolled along the lifeline in her palm.

The past twelve months had been nonstop study and preparation. Orientation Day, with the kickoff for their new class, was tomorrow. Hillary poured herself another cup of French Roast.

She couldn't go back to sleep now.

4

TUESDAY EVENING

That night, an insistent beat pulled at Hillary. It was from Claire and Keisha in the basement. Hillary hadn't appreciated their music at first, but as soon as they clued her in by chanting "We will rock you," she remembered. The *boom, boom, bap* of Queen's classic had led the rise of rap music when Hillary was a young and single twenty-something back in the '90s.

She shut her home office door, and returned to her desk, clicking through her PowerPoint slides for the class. Would she be able to confess her own failings? The collection of slides was almost ready, and the *boom-bap* flow from the basement kept knocking at her door. The girls were fine-tuning their own original hip hop creation.

Claire had caught on to kicking the drum bass

line while tapping a beat on her snare. She kept it simple to showcase Keisha's heartfelt lyrics, that often pounded out her yearning to find her mother, who'd gone missing the year after Keisha was born.

After Hillary had found her own long-lost mother last year, she had promised to help search for Tamika. So far, no luck until that piece of rope wound with chain was uncovered in the apple orchard.

No, it would be too much of a coincidence.

Now they were all ensnared in the torturous wait for the coroner's report on what exactly it was that had been found buried at Apple Acres. Or who it was. She shuddered.

Hillary closed her laptop and listened. Rap was truth-telling, set to percussion that pierced to the bone. When she heard about a rapper "sampling" bars from other artists' recorded music, the connection stood out in flashing letters. People using other people's work as their own. Sampling happened in all kinds of music.

Sampling. Plagiarism. Copyright. That gray area where lawyers played their games. There were so many ways to go wrong.

Keisha and Claire were putting together their own original creations. No sampling. They'd titled the piece they were playing now as "Gianna's Last Shot." It was a hard-hitting lament over the death of Kobe Bryant's thirteen-year-old daughter, an up-

and-coming basketball star, along with him and six others. Hillary's heart ached as she recalled seeing photos of the tragic helicopter crash taking the group to a basketball event at the Black Mamba Center.

Hillary clenched her jaw in determination. Zale had set a theme of **WAR**, *Writing about Racism*, and Hillary had focused on the critical element of crediting voices left out of history. Deliberately or accidentally. Making public so many kinds of theft. Her heart raced. Would she be able to admit her own mistakes? Was it really stealing? Using other people's words, even just a few of them? How to confess and make amends?

Tonight, she let go of her work and responded to the call of the music. With a hand on the banister, she stepped down the basement stairs and into the pounding sound. The girls had studied the music of Queen Latifah. As they watched for WNBA players to break out some albums, they'd studied local rappers like Oak Park's Mozzy. Once Hillary got past the f-words and the n- words, she related to albums like the one from NBA player Marvin Bagley, titled *JREAM*.

JREAM—a deliberate misspelling of MLK's dream. Bagley had tweeted that the title was an acronym for "Jesus rules everything around me." Hillary's friend Zale was a lay preacher and he'd said he liked hearing Bagley's profession of faith. Zale believed hip hop pieces were psalms of lament and praise, sung throughout the generations.

The rap rhythms fit into what Hillary and Zale were preparing to teach. She prayed their mix of music and messages for the new Intro to Ethnic Studies class would bring MLK's dream a step closer to reality. Even if a small step.

Closing her eyes, she embraced the music pouring from these teen-aged women she loved. She absently rubbed the Mary medal hanging from her black bead bracelet. At times like this, it was not so hard to have given up her daily glass of red wine.

5

WEDNESDAY MORNING, AUGUST 18

The August sun turned Hillary's closet-sized office into a sauna. Still, she stood at the small window shivering with excitement. On the quad below, hundreds had gathered, wide-eyed and smiling, strolling the grounds. The campus was decked out for Orientation Day in purple-and-blue banners, the college flags hanging colorful yet limp, baking in the still air.

Classes would start on campus next week, a welcome addition to the online-only offerings of the past year. The expanse of green lawn was bisected by Yokuts Creek meandering under an arched footbridge, its shadow providing refuge to the occasional trout. Uniformed campus police stood on duty, pointing out locations to new students and their parents.

Hillary's perspective was so much broader here in the Shima Administration Building from that temporary classroom where she'd taught journalism years ago. Spread out on the quad were information booths, some for classes, some for financial aid, and some for student clubs. She studied the faculty, staffing booths under the mottled shade of valley oaks, as they engaged students in the wonders of their fields of study, inviting them to afternoon presentations that would showcase details of new programs and classes.

Her faculty colleagues.

Friends and foes, from years past. She ran her fingers through her hair, pulling it from her face, a habit when she was anxious. But teaching the innovative ethnic studies class could give her a chance to redeem herself. Now, she was a different person from that young reporter overcome by panic attacks into making mistakes.

It was nearly time to kick off the introduction session for Ethnic Studies 101, Writing About Racism. WAR. Would students understand its value? Would faculty?

A knock on the door broke her reverie. It would be Zale joining her from his temporary office next door. "Come in," she said and let her hair fall free.

Grover Zale joined her at the window. "Ready for your public return?"

Her mood brightened at the sight of her friend from back when she taught at this private college. They had stayed close over the years. The sturdy scholar, an esteemed African American History professor, was coordinating a program for social justice, the brainchild of the college's new president.

Hillary tapped the windowpane with the rounded tip of a pencil eraser. "I'm afraid the faculty may not give WAR more than lip service, if even that." She rolled the pencil between her fingers and thumb, a habit from her days as a reporter. "Even though the Board approved it."

He nodded. "But as a pilot project. Don't forget that our new president," he pointed down, indicating the first floor where Booker Williams' office was adjacent to the Board of Trustees' meeting room, "has charged us with proving the value of educating all the students and not just those who already sympathize."

Hillary nodded in the direction of the Philosophy Department booth on the quad. "We'll never convince Frank Stern," she said, breathing fast. "Calls himself a Stoic, but he's a hater against the cause of community." Her breath fogged the window. She reached into the pocket of her navy blazer and pulled out a white handkerchief to rub the glass and clear the view.

Zale ran a hand over what was left of his low-cut

salt-and-pepper hair. "It's true, Dr. Stern cannot learn to accept what is happening." He chuckled. "Not as much of a Stoic as he likes to think. But no one pays him much mind, always ranting about one thing or another, clogging up the college email. The man's devoted to fighting what he sees as a left-wing plot to ruin the country. He probably won't even go to our session. It's not just old-timers like him we need to win over. It's newly tenured hot shots like his friend Nettie Kovar."

"Kovar." Hillary ran the college web page biographies through her memory, picturing photos and information about the faculty. "She teaches business?"

Zale nodded. "The entrepreneurship program. Lots of energy, that woman. She's the widow of Joseph Kovar, an organizer of the Central Valley Tea Party. As a child, she escaped communist Czechoslovakia and became a fervent follower of Ayn Rand. Nettie's made it clear she's out to shoot down ES 101."

Hillary heaved a sigh and looked for the Business Department booth.

Zale gazed over the quad and hummed quietly for a few seconds, then said, "You know we're scheduled to start at one."

Hillary turned away from the window, twisted her hair into a knot and poked in the fat pencil to hold it in place. "I want to look casual, get into a TED Talk mood for presenting WAR."

"Let's pray no one gives us a bad time before we even get started. I've heard calling it WAR makes it sound too negative. But, of course, we don't mean that kind of—" His jaw dropped.

"What's happening?" Hillary turned back to the window. A figure in a white mask zigzagged through the crowd, launching what looked like snowballs into booths and at people.

Her voice raised an octave. "People are tripping over each other, getting out of his way." She held her breath. "Over by the creek. Someone's fallen. Come on, let's see if we can help!"

She locked her office and led the way down the stairs.

At the ground floor entry, Zale said, "I was afraid … " He took a couple of shallow breaths before he carried on, "of something like this."

"Of what?" Hillary paused.

"I'll explain later," he said. "Let's go."

She pushed open the heavy glass door and rushed in the direction of shouts for help coming from the student clubs section.

Before she could take more than a half dozen steps, she was nudged aside by campus police officers, who held buzzing onlookers back while a couple of firefighters got through, EMT equipment in hand.

Zale caught up with Hillary. They threaded their way past the booths and stopped when they saw Coach Hutcheon, lying on the grass a few feet away from the Social Justice Club booth. Firefighters were working on his leg.

Several students stood watching, silent and wide-eyed. A young woman with a smooth brown complexion, her black hair formed into a bun on the top of her head, ran to Zale and hugged him. "I'm glad you're here, Professor!" She brushed tears off her cheeks. "Coach went chasing after that guy in a mask. He looked like some kind of bird. He sped away and Coach stumbled and fell!"

Zale introduced Hillary to the young woman as Neka Jay Jagdale. She gave Hillary a quick nod and tugged at Zale's arm.

Stunned, Hillary stood unmoving on the spot. She had met Bill Hutcheon fifteen years ago, when she was faculty advisor for the student newspaper. The man was a retired NBA player. He was passionate about giving all students his top-notch basketball coaching. Now he lay sprawled on the green lawn.

One of the projectile balls lay on the grass at Hillary's feet. What she'd seen on TV about preserving fingerprints crossed her mind. She took her handkerchief out of her pocket and used it to pick up the missile, the size of an orange.

With care, she opened the ball of crushed paper

enough to make out a photo and message. She carried the paper to Zale, who had walked over to a table sporting the Social Justice Club banner. On a white field in a rainbow font blazed their call to action:

Join the SoJust Club.

She offered the wrinkled paper to Zale on the tray she'd made of her handkerchief. "This is probably ridiculous but—fingerprints?"

"I'm no expert," he nodded over at the lawn dotted with crushed white balls, "but there are plenty others to get prints off." He sat at the table and smoothed the crinkled sheet out flat, with students looking over his shoulder.

As if paced by a metronome, Zale read out loud: "'Return to real learning—Ban Ethnic Studies—Make College Great Again.'" Groans and murmurs of "Oh, no!" came from the students.

The words captioned a photo of four students. He shook his head slowly before he turned to Hillary and said, "These are the leaders in our Social Justice Club." He tapped one of the faces on the crumpled page. "This one is Neka Jay, you just met. She's president this year. She got a threat yesterday. That's what I was going to tell you." His lips thinned out to a flat line.

"What kind of threat?"

"Slipped into to her mailbox in Sacramento where she lives with her parents in the Sikh community. A page torn out of a *National Geographic* magazine. It pictured Gandhi. Scrawled across it in black marker was 'Drop out of college like he did.' "

Hillary looked at Neka Jay, who said, "That was when Gandhi was young. An ignoramus sent this— no one to fear." She jerked her head to where the coach lay nearby on the grass. "I'm fine! Listen. He's talking now," she said, her voice firm. "He will be all right. He is a fighter."

In response to Neka Jay, a tepid smile was all Hillary could manage. The question was, would Coach really be all right? No one else was physically injured from this jerk streaking through the crowd tossing paper balls.

But there were other ways to be hurt. Would this young woman be all right? And the other students? She recalled the layers of shock she'd passed through when preparing for teaching the class, so many stories she had never heard before. Accounts of chaos like here today and far, far worse. But never at Clearwater, until now.

The Central Valley heat encased the quad. Hillary felt herself coming to a boil. Who could have staged this storm of paper snowballs?

She had returned to Clearwater College to help students recognize the mistakes of the past. But this hateful affront loomed larger than a mistake. The call to ban the new class just emphasized the need for ES 101.

Who would come to the presentation she and Zale were scheduled to give this afternoon? Would they be friends or foes?

6

As the tower carillon's bells signaled one o'clock, Hillary strode onto the stage in her navy blazer, a spotlight tracking her five foot eight inches, another spotlight trained on a clock face projected onto a screen behind her.

She stopped on an orange circle painted on the stage floor, pivoted to face the audience, and shouted, "It's about time!"

The clock image dissolved and in its place the acronym WAR came into focus. "I'm Hillary Broome and I've come to start WAR!" The eerie, haunting sounds of "Battle Hymn of the Republic," recorded by Jon Batiste, bounced off the walls of the auditorium.

She pulled a pair of glasses from her pocket and put them on. The lenses were coated with white paint. She pointed to them with both index fingers as if shooting herself in the temples.

A burble of surprise rose from the audience.

"You out there might be like me and wear 'color blind' glasses. At least some of the time. Or maybe not." She yanked the glasses off and put them back in her pocket.

Reaching out, she grabbed a handful of air and held her closed fist up high. "You out there might be like these five people and panic when writing." She fanned her fingers up in the direction of the screen, flashing photos of Melania Trump, Martin Luther King Jr., George Harrison, Alex Haley, and Saddam Hussein. "You may have stolen other people's words and used them as your own." The music intensified. She could see Zale motioning to her from backstage. She just wasn't ready yet.

She marched in place to the rhythm of Batiste's piano and percussion and swung her arms at her sides. "Our WAR is to arm you with education and awareness, turn you into soldiers fighting against silence, color blindness, racism and plagiarism." The acronym WAR flashed twice on the screen behind Hillary before it dissolved into words. She raised both index fingers and pointed to words she read out loud: "Writing About Racism."

The great space of the auditorium was filled with silence. Hillary used it to let the message sink in.

Her eyes measured the reactions. There was Frank Stern, at the session after all. Sitting next to him looked like that woman Zale had mentioned. Nettie something? They were both scowling.

Other faces in the audience looked as if they were stopped in time, hanging on her every word, rapt and waiting to move forward.

She had them in her pocket now. "Race. It's a concept that does not exist in nature. But racism does exist. And we are here to tackle it head-on. College students all over California," she smiled, "are first to face an Ethnic Studies requirement signed into law by California's governor."

On the screen behind Hillary, a display that read "AB 1460" throbbed for a few seconds, replaced by split-screen images of Governor Gavin Newsom at a desk, alongside an image of Grover Zale at a lectern.

Hillary nodded stage right and Zale walked out to join her. "I'm Grover Zale, in the midst of WAR." He turned to take Hillary's hand, lifting it high, as if they had just won an election. "We plan to arm you with knowledge and practice that keeps you competitive with students at the public universities in a march toward true liberty and justice for all."

The projection on the curtain dissolved into a screen shot of the Clearwater Class Schedule, showing, **"ES 101: Intro to Ethnic Studies (1 unit)."**

Zale continued. "All freshmen have been registered for ES 101. Those on campus come here, during

College Hour Thursdays at noon. Those online can Zoom in or watch the recording at their convenience."

Hillary added, "You'll write about the week's topic and we'll show examples of how to give credit to the speakers and authors."

Zale continued, "You'll gain a new sense of yourself as a powerful writer amidst the conversations and controversies of our American culture. We aim for the writing to lead you to action."

Hillary pulled out the glasses with the opaque white lenses from the pocket of her blazer and held them high. Twirling them in the air, she flung them to stage left where they skidded backstage. "It's our intention that everyone opens their eyes and discovers, as author Paul Kivel advises, 'It's Good to Talk about Racism.'"

The spotlight zeroed in on Hillary. "We hope you will come with wonder and curiosity to explore this intricate and complex issue. We encourage your feedback as we begin this journey together. Welcome to this WAR."

Hillary and Zale walked offstage to the sound of applause mixed with calls of "CRT is racism" and "Thinks she's so woke."

He whispered to her, "I thought you were going to name yourself along with the plagiarists? What about not just teaching but showing awareness of our own actions?"

Hillary ignored her friend's reminder. She couldn't stop keeping that part of herself buried, like a tattoo of shame inside her skin. Those couple of times she'd been assigned to cover a story about a bad mother .... She heaved a sigh.

Angry mutterings as people left the auditorium proved the pitch for the new class was not uniformly well received. The opposition to Writing About Racism was real. If she divulged her lapses into plagiarism, it would just give the obstructionists more ammunition.

7

FRIDAY, AUGUST 20

Late Friday afternoon, well before the sun was low enough to obstruct her vision, Nettie Kovar headed west for the faculty social, the top down on her Mercedes convertible and the ends of her blue neck scarf flying over her shoulders. With a cigarette holder clamped firmly between her teeth, she sped along the private road that bisected her acres of walnut trees, secure in knowing that Fury was supervising the younger students in finishing the essential weeding.

Once at Little Joe's Cafe, Nettie circled the block twice before pulling into a space at the curb. Parking was again challenging now that media-induced COVID hysteria was losing its grip. Business was starting to boom again, and Nettie liked it that way.

But she disliked how this event, two days after

Orientation Day, was billed as the annual faculty social. Why didn't the teachers' union call it what it was? A membership drive for the Golden West Teachers Association. The GWTA, new at Clearwater when five years ago, a misguided majority of faculty had voted for union representation.

It was a scam, Nettie thought, luring teachers into losing their uniqueness in a collective enterprise. This gathering at the end of the first week of classes was among her favorite settings to argue the virtues of the individual and the harm of the collective. Didn't they realize how much more money they could make if they returned to each one negotiating a contract on their own?

Inside the cafe, Nettie scanned the scene, taking in Joe's ever-present Day of the Dead paper cutouts strung up against the ceiling, the lacy skeleton figures dancing above the heads of the crowd. It was such a shame to cling to group identity.

But it gave Nettie a warm glow to see Frank Stern standing at the bar, his signature striped tie hugging his throat, as he held forth about his positive reasoning gospel to an adjunct faculty member Nettie didn't know. Let Frank convince that teacher of the drawbacks of unionizing, and she'd look around for someone else.

There was Grover Zale in shirtsleeves standing at a nearby table, surrounded by his Black Lives Matter followers, all lost to the appeal of reason.

Nettie searched the room for faculty new to her. She wanted to talk with independent thinkers.

But before she could start mingling in the cafe, Little Joe appeared at her side. "*Bienvenida*! We ask everyone to please wear a face covering." He pointed at the sign on the door, next to the No Smoking sign.

"Oh, I thought most places had stopped that. Please do not worry about me. I'm willing to take the risk." Nettie flashed the bright smile that often served as currency, getting her through some thorny patches.

"*Lo siento*. It's not a request," said Joe, stepping nearer to the front door. "It said on the announcement. Friends and family are invited, courtesy of the teacher's association." He held out a box of face masks.

Nettie gave a little pout. "But when you look at the statistics, masks don't really make sense," she countered.

"What happened in our family," said Joe, his brows sliding into a frown. He stretched out his other hand toward a shelf near the door. Next to a three-by-five postcard announcement of the teachers' union social, lay miniature orange chrysanthemums clustered around two small framed photos. One showed a curly-topped toddler and the other pictured two wizened elders, one with a cane and the other on a walker.

A pregnant woman came to stand by Joe's side. "*Papi*, let me handle this."

"I can deal with it, Julie." Joe raised his brows and looked Nettie straight in the eye. "We lost three to COVID." He bowed his head, nodded in the direction of the shelf and again held out the box of masks to Nettie.

"Oh, my condolences," Nettie said. "I've wanted a chance to show off my new scarf." She tucked in the ends of the stretchy blue fabric tied around her neck and slipped it up over the bridge of her nose, forming a sort of gaiter mask before she left Joe's side.

She strolled past booths along the side wall, nodding at faculty she knew. She stopped at the side of a booth holding her student Lorena and three strangers, who all looked to be in their early twenties. They had their masks pulled below their chins as they dipped tortilla chips into mounds of guacamole and swigged from bottles of beer.

One man was drinking Bohemia Clasica. It gave Nettie a start to see the label. Bohemia, her heartland, so ruined under the communists, a deep sorrow to her soul.

She lowered her face covering, introduced herself and learned that the three were second-year Clearwater students, same as Lorena, who told her, "I just applied to work in the tutor center."

"How ambitious to add that to your orchard duties! What will you be tutoring?" Nettie asked.

"Intro to Ethnic Studies now." She frowned and pursed her lips before she continued. "But later Latinx Studies."

Nettie shook her head. "It's not right to lock individuals into one-size-fits-all cages."

"I'm proud for the chance to focus on successful Latinx."

Nettie raised her eyebrows. "I hope you don't mean to disregard gender but rather to showcase entrepreneurs like the heroic Carlos Slim of Telmex?"

"Exactly!" The young woman tilted her bottle of Dos Equis in Nettie's direction. "With Carlos' foundation scholarship money, I have purchased a Zacua, an electic vehicle built in Mexico by women!"

Satisfied Lorena would lead the others down the self-starter path, Nettie directed a question to everyone at the table. "How do you feel getting back on campus?"

"It feels risky," admitted a pale, thin young man, "but I need the cash."

Nettie countered with, "Columbia and Stanford MBA programs have judged it safe to return to campus."

The young woman who had introduced herself as Neka Jay said, "Maybe safe from the virus, but might not be safe from haters running around on campus. Poor Coach," she nodded toward the back of the room. "Fortunate to come out of it with just a broken leg. He said the teachers' union is standing up for him to keep coaching from his wheelchair until he's healed."

The pale young man nodded his head and said, "The union won a raise for us part-time workers."

"Ha!" Nettie said. "Don't waste your money on GWTA dues."

At the four sets of eyes staring blankly at her, Nettie added, "They'll rob you of dollars and even worse, of thinking for yourself." She could see a light bulb going on in the pale young man's eyes, and decided she'd planted enough entrepreneurial seeds for the moment.

She excused herself and walked back to where Coach Hutcheon sat in a wheelchair. Beside him was that WAR teacher, Hillary. What a boondoggle that liberal extremist and Grover Zale had put over on the college Board of Regents. Never would have happened without that socialist new president, Williams. Things were getting out of hand. Nettie needed to marshal her forces, take a stronger stand.

Coach leaned forward. "Dr. Kovar! My worthy opponent on the union issue." He laughed. "I know you're not signing up despite my best rhetoric." He turned to look at Hillary. "But, I've convinced our returning professor here to join our team, even though she's sequestered in the admin building with management nowadays."

Hillary stretched out her hand for a shake. "Good to meet you, Dr. Kovar."

Nettie had pegged Hillary as a worthy foe of all things entrepreneurial after observing her performance in the auditorium. And here she was, impeccable in her navy blazer, her long auburn hair pulled neatly back off her face, a glass of what looked like 7Up in her hand.

Best get on her good side, show support for her efforts to improve student writing before shooting down the forced ES class. "Call me Nettie, please. I admire your leadership in stamping out theft of academic property, although not in forcing your questionable readings on all students. Still, it's exciting to see innovative on-campus productions after this pandemic shut-down."

Hillary patted the shoulder of a woman with blue-streaked white hair standing next to her. "Dr. Kovar, meet my mother, Paisley Joan. She's innovative to the max and has been volunteering in our Art Department."

Nettie shook hands with Paisley, wondering why the thin woman had fixed such a wide-eyed stare on her. Nettie turned to the coach. "I'm glad to see you out and about, Coach." She touched the edge of one of the wheels supporting his chair. "Looks like it's pretty lightweight and easy to handle. I'm hoping these wheels are temporary after your encounter with that person exercising his free speech rights."

"You must be joking? That went way past free speech," Hillary said, her narrowed eyes turning the color of flint. "Throwing those balls was a hate crime in my book and it nearly escalated to assault."

"The crowded conditions were more at fault than was the runner." Nettie smoothed the curve of her cropped hairdo. "How could—"

Paisley interrupted Nettie. "I'm hearing the voice of my grandmother. Where are you from?"

A hot mix of pride and defensiveness flooded Nettie. "What?"

"I hear that sound, the accent. My grandmother talked like that. I was told she came from Bohemia. Where are you from?"

Nettie bunched the fabric of her gaiter mask up over her nose before she spoke again. "Do you still hear it?"

"Even more so."

Nettie stepped back and pulled the fabric down. Shades of the old country still mottled her vision of freedom. She craved a cigarette but didn't dare light up. Little Joe was keeping his eye on her. A sudden weakness came over her. She looked around at the nearby tables but the chairs were all taken. She had to change the subject.

She turned to face this person named Paisley. "What have you been doing in our Art Department?"

"Setting up the Idiosyncratic Artists Show." Paisley lifted her chin and tucked her long white hair over her ear. "But I asked where you are from."

A swirl of passion rose in Nettie. She spat out the words. "Prague. I escaped communist Czechoslovakia when I was a child."

Paisley reached out for Nettie's hand. "I just learned my mother's people were from Prague. Some were Kovars."

"Kovar is my husband's name." Nettie pulled her hand away, wondering if she could be related to this outspoken artist. "My family name is Skála. Means like a rock. I had to hide in a closet while the secret police came for my parents. I stand like a rock against Ethnic Studies classes promoting collectivism."

Hillary smiled and said, "The class is about the people inside the community. It's worth fighting for if it comes to that." She half-crouched into a Karate stance, called out, "*Kiai*," and then bowed at Nettie.

"Violence is never the way," said Nettie. "I'm surprised—"

With a slam, the front door of Little Joe's Cafe burst open. Two masked figures rushed in wielding aerosol cans as if they were weapons. They pivoted and aimed the cans at the shelf by the door, holding the postcard invitation to the party and the two framed photos of Joe's family.

Nettie was speechless. She caught sight of a plaid shirt tail hanging below a black leather jacket.

The masked figures sprayed the postcard and the photos with a quick spritz of paint, then dashed out the door in a flash, leaving the crowd speechless in shock.

Little Joe stood like a statue, staring at the images of his family, erased by white paint.

The room seemed frozen in time.

A voice called out, "Maybe they're ... what's the word, taggers?"

Paisley was the first to have a semblance of rationality. She called out, "That's not the way taggers work. Taggers spray on buildings to represent where they're from or who they're affiliated with."

Hillary shouted, "This is a hate crime. Catch them!" She sped toward the front door, after Zale and a couple others had run outside chasing the two masked figures.

Nettie was stunned. Violence was never the way. She tried to recall where she'd seen that plaid shirt before. Or was it the jacket that looked familiar?

8

SATURDAY, AUGUST 21

Hillary tapped on Claire's door. No response. "Princess," she called. "Princess, you asked me to wake you up early. Can you hear me?"

Claire had been horrified to hear about the vandalism at Little Joe's Cafe. Back when they lived on their Lodi vineyard, she had loved going to his cafe, charmed by the lacy cutouts of the dancing skeletons hanging from the ceiling.

"Princess," called Hillary.

"Come in," called out Claire, in a sleep-garbled tone.

Hillary opened the door and went in to sit on the rocking chair beside Claire's bed. The room didn't really look so different over the past year. Posters of WNBA players and Claire's favorite rappers still hung from the walls.

But gone was the big dog bed for two, when Darius's mother, Daisy, had to be put to sleep. Now, his new bed was a snug fit for him in the basement amidst the four of his humans in and out all the time.

Claire was rubbing her eyes. "Thanks for waking me up, Mom, but you've got to stop calling me Princess."

"Why? What's wrong with that?"

"Well, Pillow Princess is kind of an insult."

"I just said Princess. Not Pillow Princess. What does that mean?

"It means someone who wants to lie back on her pillow, get served, not do any of the, you know, work."

"Work?"

Claire started a rocking motion under the covers.

Hillary's heart thudded. Was that what she thought it meant?

"You mean when two people are … ?"

"Yes. Having sex. You can say it, Mom." Claire sat up. "It's okay, you can say it. It's just part of life. For everyone, not just married people like you and Dad."

Claire got out of bed and hugged Hillary. "It's okay. Now let's get ready to go see if we can help at Little Joe's. I'm glad you asked if it was all right with him. Him and Julie."

Hillary marveled at how mature Claire had become. Tomorrow was her fourteenth birthday, and she had asked for a day in San Francisco in lieu of a party. Keisha and Stacy were coming along, and Paisley had even agreed to be part of the celebration.

**

When Hillary and Claire arrived at Little Joe's, he waved them to a table as his daughter Julie brought in a pitcher of *horchata* and said, "Please, share our morning refreshment."

The four of them lingered a few minutes, enjoying the creamy sweet drink before Hillary broached the topic. "I'm sorry we couldn't catch up with those kids. Did the police ever come out?" she asked.

"No," said Joe. "I called the sheriff and they said they couldn't do anything after the fact. It is just a misdemeanor, so they took a report but they don't do any investigation."

Hillary sighed. "I guess it was not a hate crime but what is called a hate 'incident.' I hope it's not connected with the class."

"Well, it was at a teachers' union event," said Joe. "Maybe it's just anti–labor union? Combined with attacking my family, makes me wonder about opposition to the farm labor union?"

Hillary frowned and nodded. "Hope we don't have any violence at the Labor Day event in Clear-water Square." She sighed again and laced her fingers through her hair pulling it up into a cascade that cooled off her neck but not her anger at the attack.

"Can't let that ruin everything, though. How do you like the *horchata*?" asked Julie. "It's a new recipe. All vegan." She poured a second round to the enthusiastic compliments.

Everyone avoided looking at the little shelf with the framed photos on it until at last Joe got up. "I saved the invitation for the party." He held out the postcard all coated with white paint. "I don't know if they were dissing the union or my people."

"Maybe both," Hillary said. "I'll take it the way it is, could come in handy, maybe."

He nodded and looked at the photos. "I have paint thinner in the shed," he gestured to the back, "but Julie can't be around it."

Julie rubbed her belly. "You can see why." She smiled but Hillary could tell she was suffering along with her widowed father.

Hillary and Claire took the framed photos out to the patio and assisted Little Joe. He poured thinner on a rag and dabbed it with care over each of the photos until the glass was clear again, making sure to not get any thinner running under the glass.

After that, he got a rag rinsed in fresh water and wiped the glass clean of all thinner smells.

They went back into the café and Joe set the photos on the colorful shelf with care. Julie returned. "Thank you, my friends," she said, tears on her cheeks.

Little Joe's stubbled chin was moist with his own tears. "Thank you for letting Julie and me see them clearly, again."

Hillary and Claire left then, and Hillary drove back to Sacramento. "That was a good start to the day," said Claire. "But now we need to call Dad and see if he found out what is happening with the rope in that orchard."

Hillary nodded. Nothing was going to slow down this daughter of hers. Hillary was going to have to work hard to keep up.

9

SATURDAY AFTERNOON

Nettie swelled with pride as she watched the double-sided pages fly out of the copier. She lifted a sheet and handed it to Fury. "Take a look at what I've got for us to hand out Thursday as students are going into and then leaving that dangerous ES 101," she said.

As he leaned against her office wall and scanned the page, she gazed at him with appreciation. He was paying close attention to every line of her Manifesto.

My Best Self Manifesto

The communism that Karl Marx promotes in his Manifesto is an idealistic phantasm, out of touch with human nature. This toxic ideology tried to delete the pronoun "I" and replace it with an implacable "we." Communism threw out individuals and replaced them with collectives. The malignant spirit of collectivism flourishes in higher education in California.

Walk away from Ethnic Studies. Turn around. Become Your Own Best Self.

I, Nettie Kovar, was born in 1975 in communist Czechoslovakia, where possession of typewriters and books was a basis for imprisonment, but my parents read to me of the American founding fathers ideals of life, liberty and the pursuit of happiness.

When I was ten, State Security police arrested my parents while I hid trembling in a closet. I was left behind with grandparents until my parents escaped, rescued me, and we emigrated to America, land of the free.

I argue that you risk nothing by refusing to participate in this morally illegitimate ES 101 class. Each of you is more than a member born inside an ethnic group you had no say in choosing.

My "Best Self" workshops provide a platform for you to list your values and goals and write your own manifesto to guide in fulfilling your potential. I encourage you to become the Author of your own life. Sign up for my workshops today.

Walk away from Ethnic Studies 101. Turn around.
Become Your Own Best Self.

**

"With this notice, you put it all in a nutshell!" Fury smiled and pointed to the window and their view of walnut trees in long rows starting twenty feet from her big house.

Nettie laughed. "A nutshell! Love your sense of humor. Please give a stack of these to others in the dorm, help me distribute them to those innocent first-year students on Thursday."

"Yes, ma'am!" He pulled at his short beard. "You don't let any grass grow under your feet, do you?"

"Grass grow?"

He rolled his shoulders and sat down. "Just slang for solving problems quickly. Directly. The way I always try and help here on your land. I've got some tricks up my sleeve to help in your mission to stop stuffing ethnic studies down everyone's throats."

Nettie pushed her chair back and walked to the window. Her land was looking better than ever now that Fury had been supervising the other workers over the past year. She had chosen him well, older than her usual work-study student and wiser, with leadership experience from the Army.

She thought back to that summer day last year when he had walked up to the house, rang the bell and introduced himself. She could tell he was hard-working and ambitious.

"Good afternoon, ma'am. Name's Walter Under-wood, friends call me Fury. Just honorably discharged from the Army. I've researched successful agriculture businesses in Northern California. Want to own my own land someday, and be honored to work for you while I take classes at Clearwater's Ag Program."

She'd invited the six-foot-tall, handsome young man into her living room, served him iced tea and her homemade chocolate chip cookies. He'd explained that he'd grown up learning about orchards from his farm-labor contractor father, following the crops.

She sensed that she could trust him, in that way she had trusted her darling Joseph. She felt a need to have this young Fury by her side. "I'd love you to join my group of work-study students for fall. They are younger than you and inexperienced at life. You could be a good role model for them."

"Why thank you, ma'am. I'd be pleased to help you train the recruits." Now he was starting his second year, leader of the others down in the barn dorm and her land had never looked better. He would help her grow the Entrepreneurship Program. Get rid of that awful forced Ethnic Studies class. Let freedom ring.

10

SUNDAY, AUGUST 22

On the drive, Claire sat in the back between Keisha and Stacy. She described in detail the places she wanted to visit for her fourteenth birthday celebration and why she was thrilled they were along with her. "San Francisco is so welcoming, for all kinds of people! I'd love to live here, someday."

Her daughter's enthusiasm for the city by the bay touched Hillary's heart. As she neared the end of the Bay Bridge, she glanced down at the Hills Brothers Coffee building and the clock tower of the Ferry Building beyond.

"Look!" called out Paisley from the front passenger seat, tapping on the window. "The Embarcadero, where artists are selling their creations. Like I was when your mother found me."

"Why don't you still do that?" Claire asked her grandmother.

"I prefer the freedom and safety of living with you all, and the use of my studio cottage in the back-yard. Artists have patrons. I have your mother."

Hillary winced at Paisley's blunt words and hoped they did not cut like a knife into Keisha, whose mother had still not been found.

"We're not going to the art market today," said Claire. "We're starting with the Seward Slides, first on my list. They were designed by a fourteen-year-old named Kim Clark. That matches me turning fourteen today!"

Claire's deft changing the subject impressed Hillary. She had researched the steep concrete slides along with Claire. "Be on the lookout for a parking place when we get to Seward Street," she said. "The slides are tucked away among ordinary houses on hillside land there. It was slated back in the seventies to become an apartment building. But neighbors got the zoning changed, and a tiny, steep park was built instead. It shows the power of people, working together."

Claire sang out, "And the slides take up most of the park! I can't wait!"

Hillary parked under a sycamore tree, and all five of them got out. Claire and Keisha pulled sheets of cardboard from the rear of the SUV.

"What's the cardboard for?" asked Stacy.

"The concrete slides slow you down. Cardboard is like a snow saucer," said Claire. She turned to Keisha. "You want to take the red or the yellow side?" She nodded toward the double entries at the top, one side topped with an arch of pipes painted yellow and the other painted red.

"I'll take red." Keisha turned to her grandmother. "We'll walk back up after and you can have a turn."

Stacy shook her head. "I don't think so. I'll be satisfied to see you survive your ride down."

Hillary laughed. "Me, too. I'll just watch from the top here." She was relieved they'd actually found Seward Mini Park hidden away in the Castro District neighborhood. She turned to Paisley. "How about you? Want to ride the hill like this?"

Paisley had pulled a sketchpad from her tote. "I'm good. Capture it on canvas later."

Claire and Keisha positioned their cardboard sheets and took the plunge, screaming for the few seconds it took to swerve against the sides, speeding down to the earthy platform at the bottom. As Hillary and the two grandmothers waited at the top, more people arrived for the adventure on this sunny Sunday. Claire and Keisha walked back up the pathway alongside the slides, laughing. "Okay, on to the other parks!" said Claire.

Hillary drove along Castro Street, the rainbow Pride flag present everywhere, on murals and even painted on the street. The red, orange, yellow, green, blue, and violet stripes reflected both the diversity and the unity of the LGBTQ community. Hillary's heart swelled with pride in her daughter, whose broad smile as she took in the sight of the Castro Theater told the story of finding the right place in the world, a place of love and support.

The Pink Triangle Park was easy to find and parking not all that troublesome. They got out and walked among the park's slim concrete columns to the rose-colored triangle in the center. A sign noted the park was designed in memory of the pink triangles that Nazis forced homosexuals to wear, sewn to their clothes in the Second World War. That infamous badge got tens of thousands killed. A sign noted that the park served as a "physical reminder of how the persecution of any individual or single group of people damages all humanity."

Hillary appreciated that the memorial statement pointed out individuals and groups, side-by-side. With quiet respect, they each took a rose-colored crystal from the triangle in the center, as the signage invited.

Back in the car, Claire held her pink crystal up against the car window and let the sun dance off its facets. Then she broke the hush. "That was so sad, the way those men were treated in the Holocaust. I've read it was different for women. There were no laws against relationships between them, but they were targeted for politics, and were also mass-murdered."

The silence in the car was palpable.

In a brighter tone, Claire said, "Now, on to Golden Gate Park. Let's find the Buffalo Paddock."

Hillary parked in her usual place next to Ocean Beach at the far end of the park. They hiked the gentle trails back in until they found the huge beasts living in an enclosed field, grazing peacefully. A baby bison ambled over near the cyclone fence. Claire held her breath in excitement for a minute before she exclaimed, "This is the best birthday present!" She had Keisha take a picture of her, outside the fencing, and the baby bison, inside, barely separated from each other. "This is such a happier ending for them! Now, I'm starving! Where's my birthday dinner?"

They walked back to Ocean Beach Cafe, its exterior decorated in the colors of the Native American Medicine Wheel. Hillary had learned that a recovering alcoholic named Joshua James had opened the restaurant and dedicated himself to building the largest non-alcoholic beverage selection in the world. He intended the place to welcome all people and serve as a place of healing.

Hillary had picked it as the perfect spot for Claire's fourteenth birthday meal.

All five of them ordered the Banh Mi Dip sandwich and a mocktail. Claire had the Virgin Mary, complete with a big stalk of celery to stir it with. Hillary stuck a candle into the tip of the celery stalk and lit it. They sang "Happy Birthday to You," while Claire finger-combed her short blond hair over her ears and beamed with happiness.

Later, they took a long walk on the sandy beach and stopped to watch the gorgeous sunset provided by the cloud-covered sky. Hillary was relieved nothing awful had happened this special Sunday, far from orchards of any kind. It had been a good day.

Ed would be home later tonight from Mississippi to surprise Claire with a birthday souvenir, but he hadn't learned anything else about the investigation yet. What kind of day would it be when they found out?

11

MONDAY, AUGUST 23

The morning sun drilled into Hillary's eyes, extra sensitive from a headache brought on by a six a.m. phone call ordering her to a meeting on campus. Her sun visor angled the wrong way to block the glare, so she placed her hand on her forehead like a baseball cap bill as she drove Highway 99 south to the college.

Halfway through Elk Grove, she spotted a billboard for Great Valley Dojo. This would be a convenient location, and she was determined to get back to practice her karate.

In the back of the Subaru Forester sat Claire and Keisha. The girls had been admitted to Clearwater College's award-winning Early Start program to move bright high school students along quickly. This achievement had underscored the wisdom of

Hillary's decision to accept the invitation to team-teach ES 101.

Now on Mondays and Wednesdays, she combined commuting to work along with taking the girls to campus for college classes, while on the other three days, Stacy would drive them to their local high school for classes and playing for the high school team.

The teens were excited they'd been allowed to register for Coach Hutcheon's ATH 110 class even though they would not play on the team, so as to not interfere with college eligibility.

Hillary was praying that Clearwater College would not be laced with the variety of hate messages sprayed on the girls' high school walls over the summer. But those paper snowballs at Clearwater had been a bad omen. She decided to prepare the girls for Coach's condition.

"Coach Hutcheon was practically attacked last week by a racist hothead who dashed through the quad," Hillary called over her shoulder.

"No way!" said Claire.

"Yes. Horrible. And he hasn't been identified either." Hillary frowned. "Coach chased him but fell down and suffered a broken leg. He was in a wheel-chair Friday, so don't be surprised if he's still in the chair," she said.

"How can he coach that way?" asked Claire.

"You've seen wheelchair basketball!" Keisha

gave a snort. "Those players better than most running on two legs."

"Coach has plenty of ways to teach," Hillary said, as she pulled into the parking lot by the Athletic Field.

She led the girls along the shortcut to the gym, past the art building where she pointed out butterflies painted on rice paper and fixed to a few window screens. Her friend Manuel had his students place them, part of the art outreach program, heralding the migration of the orange and black Monarch butterflies throughout the region.

"Monarchs!" The girls tossed imaginary basketballs into invisible hoops at the side of the building. "Go Sactown!"

Hillary laughed. The disbanded women's professional team in Sacramento had been called the Monarchs, but it was not likely to return. Maybe the butterflies would come through on migration this year, though they were on the endangered list. Hillary didn't want the girls to know she was worried whether they would be accepted by the older, more experienced students who made up the Clearwater Women's team.

Inside, Coach Hutcheon was rolling his featherweight chair across the hardwood floor. He stopped, set the brake lever and waved Hillary in. He turned to a dozen young women seated on benches below the bleachers. "Welcome to Fall 2021, Wildcats.

Joining our class are Claire and Keisha. Don't let their youth fool you. Both were on the AAU state championship team last spring."

"Know 'em," and "Hey!" called out a couple of voices. Half the young women jumped up from the bench and two of them reached out to tug Claire and Keisha over to sit with them. Hillary was glad to see how diverse the players were, in race, size, and apparent social background.

Enthusiastically, Coach explained that his lectures would be in the morning while they'd have practice in the afternoon, so as to let them attend other classes in between.

Hillary relaxed. Claire and Keisha would be fine. She reminded herself that at fourteen and fifteen, they were already being scouted by programs like UConn and Notre Dame. They were going to feel at home here, fit in well.

12

SMALL Day

Hillary was tense and nervous about the upcoming meeting called by the Dean of Instruction. The woman had been in a panic. It seemed a growing number of students were texting and emailing her office, protesting Ethnic Studies 101 listed on their schedules when they had not registered for it.

"We need to discuss this issue," Van Cleese had said. "It puts the new class in jeopardy. I was in support at first but I'm having second thoughts. I've asked a few others to meet this morning in my conference room."

Hillary had disconnected the call and groaned loud enough to wake Ed. He slid his arm under her shoulders and gathered her to his side. "What's wrong, Chickadee?"

There it was again. His nickname for her. She was going to have to explain the problem to him, but this was not the right time. Ed looked too cute in his early morning vulnerability, and she didn't want to dive into complexity at the moment.

"It's that crazy Van Cleese. She argued against the class from the start. And she's a naysayer from years ago when she was a tight-ass academic researcher." Hillary pulsed with energy. She hugged Ed tight and jumped out of bed. "I've got to go battle a bureaucrat."

**

Hillary located Dean Van Cleese's small conference room with no trouble even though it was at the other end of the admin building from Hillary's tiny space. A tad out of breath, she entered the conference room to find Van Cleese at the head of the table, as if posing for a painting in her institutional glory, surrounded by underlings. Hillary took the chair next to Grover Zale and across from Nettie Kovar and Frank Stern, who had his hands on a stack of books.

On the walls hung prints from American history: the signing of the Declaration of Independence, George Washington crossing the Delaware and Betsy Ross hand-stitching the original American flag. Next to the door was a poster enumerating Benjamin Franklin's Thirteen Virtues.

Hillary nodded pointedly at the framed works on the walls and said, "Interesting decor." Zale rolled his eyes. This is what's wrong in education, Hillary thought. This one-sided view of our history. All these old white people on the walls, boxing everyone in.

Van Cleese scraped her chair back and stood as tall as her five feet, two inches would allow. She pressed her hand to her bosom and said, "Thank you for coming on such short notice. There appears to be an issue over the new Ethnic Studies 101." She patted a stack of printouts on the table in front of her. "I have called for faculty consideration of the course, in the spirit of full transparency."

She pursed her thin lips into a tiny rosebud and cleared her throat before she continued. "Last year, our Board of Regents may have been intimidated by public opinion when they approved this hastily designed pilot project. They were, perhaps, swayed by activists and the enthusiasm of our new President Williams, in his outreach for student enrollment."

"I wouldn't put it that way," said Hillary. "It's that with the hate crimes shown every day on the news, people, including our Board, are waking up to the problems of systemic racism."

Zale spoke up. "Yes, and our Board voted to mirror implementation of AB 1460. All Cal State students starting this semester must take an Ethnic Studies class to graduate. You know that, Lavender. We are merely piloting a mandatory *introduction* to the subject."

"Well," Van Cleese folded her arms below her bosom and took a deep breath before she continued, "many of our students want an education simply for a career, that sort of thing. They shouldn't all have to take ES 101." Her voice took on a softer tone as she carried on with her points. "Our Board went along with this six-week class due to Hillary's mixing it with improving student writing, under the guise of teaching to give credit to sources and avoid academic dishonesty." She smiled slowly and looked at Hillary for a response.

"It's not that different from mandatory programs for first-year students at other colleges," Hillary said, leaning forward, a flush rising to her cheeks. She had to play this right, to stick to the facts and leave emotion out of the discussion ... for now.

"You realize that our students don't even all have to write, not in the English Department way." Van Cleese's voice took on a hard edge. "I admit this whole idea is bothering me now that I've had more time to let it sink in. For one thing, why does 'ethnic studies' only mean certain ethnicities?"

Her cheeks heating with anger at the dean's attitude, Hillary kept her voice as calm as she could. "We focus on the groups most harmed, historically speaking, which data was provided to the Board before their vote," countered Hillary.

Van Cleese's volume rose. "Why is there an assumption that being white in the U.S. is not an ethnicity? Why is someone whose ancestors came to this country in 1700 called an African American but someone like me whose ancestors came from Scotland around that same time is just called an American?"

Hillary was stunned at the passion coming from the woman, generally so proper in her communications, now so unprofessional. What was worse, she was posing a threat to the life of the class Hillary and Zale had worked on with such serious dedication.

Frank nodded vigorously. "I agree, Dr. Van Cleese. There is overt racism in the very roots of this class." He pulled a book out from those he'd set on the table and waved around a copy of Adam Smith's *The Wealth of Nations*. "It's better to teach students to live by truth, ideas that have stood the test of time."

Hillary sat back, trying to remain calm. "In ES 101, we're providing students with information to understand how race is intertwined in history, then to use that knowledge to think and write about current issues they face all around them now."

Nettie Kovar leaned forward. "Student writing can use a lot of help, it's true," she said. "Still, that does not have to be mixed with ethnic studies. Writing is also needed in business. The entrepreneur holds up the world, and he can be of any color." She lifted her chin.

Hillary almost choked. Where in the hell was that woman coming from?

"I myself am proud to be color blind," pronounced Frank, straightening his shoulders. "It's not necessary to squeeze the individual into a group in order for him to pursue a good life." He tapped the cover of the book at the top of his stack, picturing a marble sculpture of a man.

"You just want to sell more of your personal improvement books," retorted Hillary, "yet you refuse to see that in our culture, the system is set up on an uneven playing field." She turned to Van Cleese. "Coming here and living by choice is different from being kidnapped and shipped over as an enslaved person." Her heart raced. What was wrong with these people, so proud of being blind?

Nettie brushed her short black hair off her cheek and carried on in dulcet tones. "In addition, the way things are structured now, many individuals are harmed by minorities receiving unearned advantages. Ayn Rand said those who deny individual rights cannot claim to be defenders of minorities."

"Affirmative action is not unearned advantage," said Zale. "It is one step to making up for centuries of persecution."

Lavender Van Cleese cleared her throat loudly. "President Williams asked me to tell you he's reminding the Board to continue giving ES 101 a fair chance," said Van Cleese. "He made that clear even after I told him I'm tabulating complaints from students. And from their parents and other stakeholders around here."

She patted the stack of printouts on the table. "If opposition keeps building, something will need to be done. Clearwater's mandatory ES 101 might have to be changed. We may have to make it optional."

Zale scooted back his chair and stood. "That will cancel the benefits. Look around you, for example." He extended his arms the length of the table. "How many people of color were invited to sit here today?"

Van Cleese stared at Zale, her jaw clamped shut. There was a long moment of silence.

"But," said Frank, "what if after the ES 101 Intro, students take the ethnic studies class connected to their own culture? They already know about that. They should have a variety of options and freedom to choose among them."

"That's another benefit of ES 101," said Hillary. "It starts with the four areas mandated but the new law, but also touches on LGBTQ folks, Muslims and the hidden costs of oppression to everyone."

Zale nodded and sat back down. "ES 101 is not so different from New Student Experience programs required for freshmen at other colleges," he said. "And it will help increase registration for the regular Ethnic Studies classes. Most of them are late-start to fit student schedules after they finish 101."

Hillary gestured at the images of powerful people from history decorating the conference room's walls. "ES 101 can be one small step leading to repair of inequities caused by past persecution."

"I'm preparing a different option," said Nettie. "I'll be making it public in a few days."

"Can you give a hint?" asked Hillary. What could this Tea Party widow have in her quirky mind?

Nettie lifted her chin, offered a broad smile and said no more.

Van Cleese stood, took a deep breath and folded her arms beneath her expanded chest. "That's all for today. I wanted to put you on notice. It is clear we may need to consider how to proceed in light of growing opposition to ES 101."

Hillary walked out of the room behind Zale, feeling more determined than ever. In three days, they would be presenting the first Writing About Racism class. ES 101 would be webcast as well and recorded for students who'd chosen the online option.

She and Zale spent the next few hours in the auditorium, getting their stage props and technological ducks in a row. There was a lot riding on this first session. They had to make it a success for all the students. Hillary didn't want to consider what might be lost if the pilot project class failed to become permanent.

13

SAME DAY

At four, Hillary left the auditorium for the gym and caught the end of basketball practice. From the sideline, Coach blew his whistle and yelled, "Great hustle on defense today! Off you go!" The sweaty players ran to the locker room.

Coach rolled near to where Hillary sat on the bleacher. "Claire and Keisha make some of my college players look like first graders."

Hillary warmed to the compliment for her daughter and Keisha. "Good to see you bouncing back from that incident on the quad."

"Never seen the likes of that here in the past." He shook his head. "I don't really need the chair." He bent to yank at the top of a rigid walking boot on his right foot. "But while I've got new footwear on, this featherweight lets me speed around fast, plus I get to learn what it's like to be in a chair. Helps out with advising the SoJusters. The club gets students in chairs some semesters."

Hillary nodded. "I don't know how you have time to advise the club with all you do here." She waved her hand to embrace the space of the gym.

"It means a lot to me, my small part to making the world a better place for my wife and family, to tell the truth. Kind of selfish of me, but ... "

"Your wife. I never met her. Was she at the faculty party?"

"Phyllis was busy babysitting our twin grandbabies, Rashad and Ayani."

Hillary smiled. "Grandbabies, how sweet. I notice you have a player here named Ayani, too."

Coach beamed. "One of my best guards. She and your Claire, both with the talent to get to the top. Glad to see you back at Clearwater, leading such an important project as ES 101."

Hillary nodded. Coach's expectation of her success added to the weight of her own expectations of herself.

**

Backpacks slung over their shoulders, Claire and Keisha joined Hillary for the walk to the parking lot. "I did the right thing, cutting my hair," said Keisha, running her hand over her close-cropped tight black curls.

Claire grinned and finger-combed her straight blond pixie cut down over her ears. "I bet we could make it onto the men's team."

"We better than them."

Hillary led the way down a path marked by rows of sycamore trees, their bark peeling off in puzzle-piece shapes and a few of their big caramel-colored leaves starting to fall. At the sound of a rustle from the tree limbs, Hillary looked up, expecting to see a bird, maybe even a nest though she knew it was too near the end of summer to hold fledglings.

What she spotted instead horrified her.

Two figures dressed in baggy shorts and tiny sleeveless jerseys were hanging by the neck from white strings. She blinked a few times to make sure she wasn't seeing things. A miniature lynching. The two figures reminded her of Ken and Barbie dolls in the worst way.

Who would have done this? Was it related to those snowballs last week on the quad? To spray-painting over Little Joe's family photos? Should she point these awful figures out to Claire and Keisha?

No. Way too horrible to experience on their first day of class.

She hurried the girls on toward the parking lot, her face hot with shame over not knowing what was the right thing to do.

**

Late that night breezes flowed up from San Francisco Bay to lift the heat of the day off the valley. Hillary sat on the edge of the bed and turned to look at her husband. Ed had already stretched out his lanky frame under the lightweight top sheet.

"Something awful happened on campus today," she said and described leaving the gym with Claire and Keisha for the drive home. She traced the scalloped hem of the sheet between her thumb and forefinger before she looked up and pointed at the ceiling. "I found little black dolls, hanging in a tree. By strings. Lynched. In basketball uni's."

"Jesus." Ed sat straight up. "We get incidents like this all over town," he said, his voice rising. "Southbridge Private Security sent us to a conference on this issue just last week. I hate to see it down at Clearwater, too. You reported it, right?"

"Shhh." She nodded toward the hall. "I don't want Claire to hear this. I haven't told anyone yet. I didn't want the girls to witness that horrible sight on their first day."

He frowned. "You should have notified campus police then and there," he carried on in a lower tone. "And Claire. She needs to be prepared for the reality down there. Keisha knows about this from her life experiences."

Hillary shook her head slowly. "It was right

outside the gym. I'm afraid it's a warning against Coach and his basketball programs."

Ed stood and pointed at her. "It's a hate incident, plain and simple. Not a hate crime, but headed in that direction." His tone softened. "I know you wish this were a better world, and this conference introduced me to a new way to work on that I'll tell you about when we get more time. But for now, you need to notify campus police."

She heaved a deep sigh. "But I think Coach needs to know about it first, see how he wants to handle it. Keep it from the girls if possible."

He shook his head. "No. It needs to be reported to the law. Right away. And you know the girls will find out sooner or later."

Hillary's shoulders slumped and the corners of her mouth turned down. She said nothing as she traced the half circles of the sheet's scalloped edges with her fingernails.

"Okay," Ed said, "tell Coach first thing tomorrow." He sat back down on the bed and leaned over to smooth her pillow. "And make sure after you tell him, you go report it. Do the right thing, Chickadee.

When they first met, she loved his nickname for her, but she'd learned the tiny black, white and tan bird was a symbol of positivity, happiness and good luck, representing truth and knowledge for some Native American tribes. She had to set him straight. "I know you mean it in all kindness and fun, but calling me Chickadee is appropriating the term from Native American culture, like stealing almost, and you don't mean to do that."

Ed's eyes took on a twinkle. "How did you know? We touched on that topic at the conference! Bet you forgot that my given name is Odgar, Welsh for the Old English Edgar. It means 'wealthy spear' of all crazy things." He laughed and thrust his arm in the air. "So I'll give you a new name when the right one comes to me. How's that?"

Exhausted, she gazed into his eyes, the startling blend of jade green and turquoise that still sent out thunderbolt energy like when they first met nearly twenty years ago. "Let's forget about words for now." She slid in under the sheet, loving her husband and feeling just the right amount of warmth on this hot summer night.

14

TUESDAY, AUGUST 24

The next morning, Stacy picked up Claire to drive the girls over to high school for the day. Hillary headed down to the college where she planned to report the dolls to campus police and later meet in Zale's office to create slides for the next class session.

Hillary found the tiny dolls still hanging in the same place. Her stomach clenched at the grim tableau. "Damn racists," she muttered, feeling ashamed she'd not reported them earlier, so they could have been taken down. It didn't seem as if anyone had noticed them though.

She took a couple of pictures with her phone, in case that would be useful later. Coach would be busy, getting the fall athletics programs started, but still she wanted to tell him before she reported it to the campus police.

Hillary found Coach on the basketball court, letting the men's team go after their practice. "Looks like those wheels aren't slowing you down any," she said. "Do you have a few minutes?"

"Sure. What's up?" He fastened his pen to the top of his clipboard.

"I hate to tell you this, but I found something awful just outside your gym yesterday."

"My gym." Coach tapped his finger on the clipboard and waited for her to go on.

It took a couple seconds before she could spit out the words describing the tiny figures hanging high in the sycamore tree outside.

"Jesus," he whispered, his fair skin blanching. "Who would have done this?"

She shook her head. "It's awful. I'm on my way to the campus police, but I thought to tell you first."

Coach scanned the cavern of the court. "It's up to us to wake up more people."

"That's what we're trying to do with ES 101," Hillary said.

"It's not enough." Coach smacked his clipboard with the flat of his hand. "It's not enough! I'm asking you to get involved in the student SoJust club. I'm their advisor but we need more faculty support. Come to the meeting this afternoon. Tell them what you saw."

**

Hillary crossed back over the footbridge to the one-story, gray stucco Public Safety building. She was familiar with its purpose but had never gone inside before. Once there, she said, "I need to report a hate incident," to the officer at the front desk.

The young woman gestured for Hillary to have a seat, turned to the computer on her desk and started typing. "I can take your report in just a moment," she said.

Hillary looked out over the large space furnished with black steel desks. A door at the back opened and several men in campus police uniforms plus a couple in county sheriff garb left what looked to be a conference room.

Zale's husband, Dupree, was among them. She knew he was an FBI agent, and she was surprised to think that the FBI would have stepped in already. Still, it was understandable that Dupree would want to keep an eye on the college, maybe in an informal way.

She stood and gave him a quick wave. He came up to the front desk. "What brings you here, Hillary?"

"It's a horrible thing I found yesterday over by the gym. It's not a hate crime, but it should be. I think it's called an incident."

"What was it?" asked Dupree.

"In a sycamore tree outside the gym, two tiny dolls, hanging from strings tied to the branches."

Dupree blew out a long breath. "Still there?"

"Just now, yes."

"I'll get a couple campus cops to go with me, document the scene and take them down. Have you told Zale?"

"Not yet," Hillary said, raking her fingers through her hair and letting it fall to her shoulders. "But I'm going to, right after I finish giving my report." She shook her head in sorrow at the same pace as Dupree shook his own.

Twenty minutes later, Hillary went to Zale's office. He was busy editing their slides for the first class session.

Zale was astounded to hear about the dolls. He pounded his fist on the desktop. "Lord! A lynching on campus!"

"Right outside the gym, too," she said. "Looks like it's directed against Coach and student athletes. You know my daughter and her friend are in Coach's class as part of the Early College program."

"Times seem to be worse lately, so related to the sermon I'm writing for next Sunday."

"Really?"

"Based on a book I've meditated on for years."

"Coach told me he wanted me to do more, be more active, get involved in the student club. What is your relationship with those students?"

"They feel at home meeting in my history class-room. I'm not formally an advisor, but want to do all I can to support them. It looks like we might combine forces with the club to strengthen the class."

Hillary nodded. "Some club members are working as TAs for the class."

"It's a growing community."

**

At 3:00, Hillary went to the Social Justice Club meeting. They met in the classroom where Zale taught his courses. The old wooden desks had been moved to the perimeter of the room, except for those in a circle in the center, with an open space where she expected Coach to position his wheelchair.

She noticed a young woman wearing a black T-shirt that read on the back:

So Just
what are
Jewish markers?

* **G**od is and rules
* **G**od is One
* **G**od created the world
* **C**reation is One
* **G**od's Providence rules creation

On each desk was an agenda stating the club's mission, centered at the top. Hillary scanned the printout and noted an action item listed "SoJust T-shirt sales update." That must account for the Jewish markers T-shirt.

A young man wore one that proclaimed Muslim markers in a tiny font as:

- ◆ PROFESSION OF FAITH (SHAHADA)
- ◆ PRAYER (SALAT) DAWN, NOON, MID-AFTERNOON, SUNSET, AFTER DARK
- ◆ ALMS (ZAKAT)
- ◆ FASTING (SAWM)
- ◆ PILGRIMAGE (HAJJ)

Below the T-shirt–update agenda item was one that said: "CHANGE CLEARWATER DRIVE TO BLACK LIVES MATTER AVENUE."

Hillary was struck by the impressive action goals of this group, so aligned with the aims of ES 101. Or was it vice versa?

As she waited for the meeting to start, Hillary studied the collection of posters hanging on a wall that had been painted a stop-light green.

One poster showed the legendary contralto Marian Anderson dressed in a magnificent off-the-shoulder gown, her words in quotes below her image:

"No matter how big a nation is, it is no stronger than its weakest people, and as long as you keep a person down, some part of you has to be down there to hold him down, so it means you cannot soar as you might otherwise."

Amen, thought Hillary.

**

Coach arrived, got himself situated, and president Neka Jay led the roll call. Most students responded with a simple "Here," but at the name Lorena Vaz, a young woman hissed her response, "Presente."

Her dark eyes sparkling, Neka Jay introduced Hillary. "Most of you know Professor Broome, who is co-teaching the Ethnic Studies Intro. We are happy over this new support for our vision of justice for all. Welcome, Professor Broome!"

Hillary took a deep breath and drew herself up to her full height, trying to make space for the butterflies in her stomach.

She nodded at the slim figure of Coach in his wheelchair, his pen poised over a clipboard, and she took a few seconds to smile at the young people in the room, appearing to mirror Clearwater's diverse student population.

Her blood ran cold over what she was about to

do, describe the tiny lynched figures to this group, so passionate about social justice. There were two Black students in the room. Could they have been the target of those dolls? An effort to intimidate? Her stomach burned.

"I admire your strong presence here, Neka Jay, standing undaunted over the hateful message to you last week wrapped up in those paper snowballs."

Unsmiling, Neka Jay bobbed her head, her black bun on top jiggling a bit.

"What I don't admire is what I saw yesterday on our campus, over by the gym." Hillary waited a few beats before going on. "It was a demonstration of why your work in this club is so important. It was the exact opposite of all you are striving for." Now the students were wide-eyed, waiting. "It was two tiny dolls dressed in basketball uni's, strings around their necks, hanging from the branches of a tree."

Gasps and cries of "No!" rang around the room. Two students stood, shaking their fists. One of them yelled, "That's awful!" The other said, "What did you do?"

"I reported it to campus police, who were already working with the FBI over the snowball chaos last week. The dolls have been taken down and processed as evidence. So keep your eyes open: if you see something, say something."

Hillary smiled before she went on. "You and your group are part of making things better. I admire you and the artwork on your green wall," she said, gesturing toward the posters.

"We change it up to keep it fresh," said Neka Jay. "We call it our 'Green means Go' wall."

Hillary nodded. "And I applaud your role in getting the bathrooms changed to Gender Neutral and your plans to propose that the Board rename Clearwater Drive as Black Lives Matter Avenue," she said.

"We didn't agree on that," called out Lorena Vaz.

"The rename project passed by a vote at the end of the spring semester, Lorena," said Neka Jay. "It's in the minutes." She placed her palm on a binder on her desktop and turned to a young man sitting next to her. "Bayani will read the minutes soon."

"I was absent when you pushed it through." Lorena scowled. "I was gone to Mexico for the summer. Visit with my family. Shouldn't be punished for that."

"There was a quorum that day, so I'm sorry if you were not here, but we did approve the plan." Neka Jay gazed steadily at Lorena.

"I'm sick and tired of this mob rule," shouted Lorena. "Forget about my offer to make fried ice cream on Labor Day."

Hillary was surprised to see the young woman stand and fling her thick braid over her shoulder. She grabbed her backpack and marched to the door.

"Muchedumbre," she called over her shoulder as she pulled open the heavy door and left.

Hillary lifted her eyebrows and looked at Coach and then at Neka Jay, but neither commented. A couple students mirrored rolling their eyes at each other.

"Fried ice cream wasn't practical, anyway," said Angel.

Neka Jay carried on, ticking off agenda items. At the Labor Day event item, she noted that at the end of last semester, they had obtained a permit to march and reserved a space in the Clearwater town square.

She asked for ideas from the group. Bayani talked about holding a potato sack race to give the experience of how the playing field was not even. Other students expressed their ideas, but they couldn't agree on a plan.

"We need to commit to action," emphasized Neka Jay. "Our SoJust Identi-tee shirts are due to arrive for us to wear in the march, but they aren't really action." She gestured toward the classroom's single green wall. "Don't forget why we painted it green. It's for 'go,' remember. Go make change happen. Don't just talk about it."

Action, thought Hillary. The purpose of information was to move to action.

15

THURSDAY, AUGUST 26

From her position backstage, Hillary peeked out into the Shima Auditorium. It was nearly one o'clock. The plan was for Neka Jay and other club members to greet students in the foyer as they arrived and give each a handout, pointing to where to write on the handouts. Students were to use their ID numbers instead of their names, to give them the freedom to write with maximum honesty.

Lorena had backed out, saying she objected to the mandatory aspect of ES 101. Lorena's action had made Hillary begin to reconsider the recommendation process for the young woman's tutoring application.

ES 101 had been assigned the largest hall on the Clearwater campus. Due to the pandemic, more than half of the students had taken the online option, still Hillary knew there should be a large number for the in-person class.

She pulled her handkerchief from her blazer pocket and wiped perspiration from above her lip, giving more time for the hall to fill. At one minute past the hour, she nodded at the student working the electrical panel. The ambient lights flickered and went out.

Hillary and Zale led a version of the WAR theme they'd presented on Orientation Day. Then directions were projected on the huge screen set up in front of the red velvet curtain.

WHEN THE LIGHTS COME BACK ON,
TAKE FIVE MINUTES TO WRITE DOWN
WHAT YOU THINK CAUSES WARS.

The lights came on. The faint sound of a ticking metronome began. Hillary watched as some students stared into space, others frowned and whispered but most began writing furiously.

At the five-minute mark, the lights went out. A YouTube video filled the screen. It was the reggae artist Bob Marley performing his song, "*War.*"

Eyes closed, he stomped to the energy of the music, surrounded by his band on drums, keyboard, and guitars. Women in headwraps of green, red, yellow, and black swayed to the music.

Zale stood motionless throughout the video, but

many students kept time to the beat with heads bobbing and shoulders rocking.

Hillary nodded along with Marley's rhythmic slaps on the backbeat, but she was concerned to see a few students glaring with sullen faces and narrowed eyes. *Got to get them to understand why this matters. It's a global issue.*

The video ended and there was a second of silence before lights flooded the auditorium. Projected onto the screen were Bob Marley's lyrics:

"UNTIL THE PHILOSOPHY WHICH HOLDS ONE RACE

SUPERIOR

AND ANOTHER INFERIOR

IS FINALLY

AND PERMANENTLY

DISCREDITED

AND ABANDONED

EVERYWHERE IS WAR.

ME SAY WAR

THAT UNTIL THERE'RE NO LONGER

FIRST-CLASS AND SECOND-CLASS CITIZENS OF ANY NATION

UNTIL THE COLOUR OF A MAN'S SKIN

IS OF NO MORE SIGNIFICANCE THAN THE COLOUR OF

HIS EYES

ME SAY WAR"

Zale walked out onto the stage. At the side of the screen, he reached up and touched the bottom corner, causing the huge sheet of white vinyl to vibrate. Looking up at the lyrics, he began reading the words in a slow, loud voice, line by line, very different from the way Bob Marley had performed it. And very clearly.

"Now," he said to the students, "underneath your own opinion of what causes wars, take five minutes to write Bob Marley's opinion of what causes wars. Start your writing by noting that in his song titled 'War,'" Bob Marley suggests that the cause of war is ....

"Then either write his exact words from the song in quotation marks or put his ideas into your words but name him as the source."

Hillary stepped out from behind the curtain and walked near stage front and center. "Giving credit for their words is one way to stop stealing from people. Stop the appropriation of ideas from those who have been disadvantaged by systems in power."

Zale nodded. "After you credit Marley for his words, turn your handout over and on the back side, explain how similar or different your opinion is from Marley's. Quote a few words from his lyrics in your writing. Use the information on the screen to practice in-text citation and reference style required for ethnic studies classes."

Hillary, Neka Jay and other TAs walked up and down the aisles and stopped to answer questions and offer suggestions to students having difficulties with the assignment.

A few students were not writing anything on their handouts but Hillary decided to ignore that for this first session and reinforce the positive responses.

On the stage, Zale addressed the students. "I hope you got a lot from Bob Marley's performance. He was awarded the International Peace Medal by the African delegation to the United Nations in 1978. His life demonstrates many connections between war and peace."

Hillary joined him on stage as a different image was projected onto the screen. "Today, you've seen Marley bring up the topic of first- and second-class citizens. Separating people into privileged and oppressed groups happens all around the world as described in the book titled *Caste* by Isabel Wilkerson."

Hillary gestured up at the screen. "Here you see an image showing America's caste system, where people are pressed into categories. We all carry stereotypes of these categories around with us."

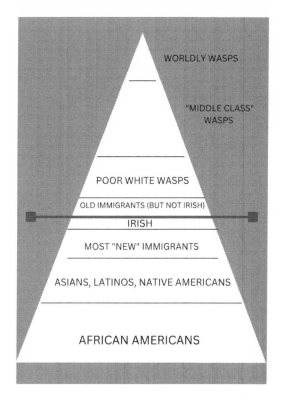

Zale waited a few minutes to let students study the image, before he spoke. "ES 101 uses stereotypes as subject matter along with reading and writing about them. The homework for next week is to bring in a written description of two stereotypes you see in this coming week. Even better, if you catch yourself in the act."

Hillary added, "This class is not just about writing. It's also about actions, sometimes very small but powerful actions. For example, I've been paying attention to when I use stereotypes, noticing them, talking about them. It can help in becoming more aware."

Zale concluded in his calm, strong preacher's tones, "Finish up your comments then print your student ID number at the bottom and turn your handout in to a TA. You will find it next week sorted by ID numbers on the foyer tables. It will have our comments on it for you."

Hillary smiled and said, "Class dismissed. We'll see you outside afterwards and be glad to chat if you have any questions."

Would anyone take the time to ask questions?

16

SAME DAY

Hillary stood outside the auditorium doors as students streamed out, headed down the broad stairway to the quad. The first ones hurried across the green grass, now empty of Orientation Day booths and decorations, the white snowballs held as evidence, Hillary had learned.

She was more than surprised to see Nettie Kovar at the bottom of the stairs. It looked like she was passing out some kind of advertising flyers. Near her were two young people who seemed to be handing out the same things. Pushing them out was more like it.

A couple of students glanced at the single sheet shoved at them and tossed it into the recycling bin.

Hillary walked down the concrete stairs. "What's going on?" she asked Nettie.

Nettie handed her a flyer at the same time as she smiled and thrust a copy into the hands of a student just stepping off the stairway. Nettie turned to Hillary, pointed to the top of the single-spaced document and read out loud, "'My Best Self Manifesto,'"

"A Manifesto? What's that doing here?" Hillary scanned the sheet.

"It's to stand up for choice, an alternative to your forced ES 101."

"An alternative?" Hillary's low tone masked her anger.

"This is America, land of the free. I am inviting students to select reason instead of being herded, like brainless sheep. To use their critical thinking. Isn't that what college is supposed to teach?" She stretched out a flyer to a passing student, who took it and stopped to look it over.

"You can't do that," Hillary said. "This is a required class for all first-year students. All of them." She turned to Zale, who had just come down the steps and joined them, a frown on his face. "Did you hear what Dr. Kovar said?"

"I did. And you're way out of line, Dr. Kovar."

Nettie laughed. "Before the two of you started your ES 101 session today, I already diverted some individuals to my kind of ES, an Entrepreneurial Studies workshop. Didn't you notice the auditorium was not as full as you expected?"

A young man with a beard shouted up at students still coming down the steps, "Critical Race Theory is racist!" as he handed out flyers.

A few young people stopped on the stairs, listening. "You crazy racist," a petite redhead yelled down at Nettie. "We need Ethnic Studies. What's wrong with you?" She tore her flyer in half and half again and threw it at the bearded young man.

Nettie retorted, "Take control of your life."

"She's right! Black Lives Matter mobs want to take over the country," shouted a young woman, her blond ponytail flicking from side to side as she handed out flyers to curious students gathering around. "We've got as much free speech as the Marxists," she yelled.

Hillary was stunned at the size of the growing crowd. Many students had diverted and about-faced to see what the shouting was about. Hillary was glad to see campus police officers making brisk headway toward the gathering that looked to number nearly twenty, some jostling for a better view of Nettie and her students with the armloads of flyers.

Another officer joined the crowd just as Coach Hutcheon rolled up in his featherweight wheelchair. "What's happening? Looks like one of those European soccer matches that ends up in a riot."

"Dr. Kovar here," Hillary narrowed her eyes at Nettie, "wants to use a manifesto to pull students away from Intro to Ethnic Studies. She doesn't think Writing About Racism supports the individual."

"No, it does not, you've got to acknowledge that," said Nettie.

"The individual!" Coach looked up at Nettie. "There's no 'I' in team. Too many self-centered egotists are shouting out now. That's what we need to combat." He reached into the pack at the back of his wheelchair, pulled out a small orange megaphone and addressed the gathering crowd. "Calm down, folks! Carry on to your classes."

The bearded young man strode over beside Coach. "Stay out of this, old man. No one needs brainwashing to get sucked into defunding the police." He nodded in the direction of the campus police officers, now nearby.

"No one mentioned anything about that," Coach replied.

"We are fine," said one of the campus officers.

"You won't be after these two," the bearded young man gestured toward Hillary and Zale, "get done pushing their Critical Race Theory. Take a look at one of these." He held his stack of flyers out in front of the officer.

The officer put one hand on the stack of flyers and his other on the young man's shoulder. "Take it easy," he cautioned.

"The hell I will." The young man twisted away from the officer, his flyers swirling to the stairway.

He reached for them, lost his balance, and grabbed at the handle of Coach's wheelchair.

The featherweight chair tilted.

It tumbled backwards onto the auditorium steps. Appalled, Hillary watched it fall as if in slow motion.

The back of Coach's head smacked against the concrete steps with a dull and heavy *thwack*, the megaphone falling from his hand and bouncing away.

Hillary screamed, her scream echoing in the air, in her brain, as if it would never stop.

The officer gripped the young man's hand and pulled him to his feet. He stood, pivoted on his heel and started to walk away. The officer reached out and took hold of the man's shoulder to detain him. The young man stopped and stood still. Another officer moved in, calling the crowd to stand back.

Hillary knelt beside Coach and stared in horror as a drop of blood from the back of his head spread into a small dark circle on the concrete. "Got to..." he gasped.

"Stay with me," Hillary urged, her throat tight. "Call 911," she yelled.

"Take..." He lay still, barely breathing as a siren blared from a distance. He managed a faint word, "Club," and then he went limp.

She felt for his carotid and detected a weak pulse.

Hillary kept repeating, "Stay with me, Coach, stay with me." She ran her handkerchief lightly across his forehead and tickled his cheeks with the corners of the white fabric. "Stay with me!"

A couple of campus police parted the crowd as EMTs rushed in to work on Coach.

Zale stood a few feet away with his eyes closed, rubbing the tiny brass cross hanging from a chain around his neck. Hillary held her breath, hoping to see Coach move, even just twitch a finger. But nothing. With her hand cupping her cheek, Hillary watched as Coach lay fallen. There was nothing to do but to watch.

Neka Jay came and sat by her side on the concrete step, tears streaming down both of their faces.

Then Coach let out a moan.

17

SAME DAY

Hillary and Neka Jay, silent and frowning, took in the aftermath of the turmoil. After what felt like forever, the EMTs transported the barely responsive Coach into their ambulance and drove off. The crowd wandered away in clusters of two or three, heads bent together, looking back at the scene.

The same two campus police officers were still talking to the bearded young man, by himself and empty-handed now. Nettie and the young blond woman were walking away, toward Highway 99.

To Hillary's shock, the officers let the young man go. He left campus, headed in the same direction as Nettie. Hillary shook her head. "Why are they letting him go?"

Neka Jay shrugged. "You know the way it goes. Accidents happen."

Hillary's eyes bulged. "He caused someone to get hurt! It was the same way with those snowballs on the quad! And even the spray painting at Little Joe's Café! They shouldn't just let him go!"

"Well, he's white. That's just one example of what we are up against."

Hillary scowled. "Where is Dr. Kovar going?" she asked Neka Jay.

Neka Jay narrowed her eyes and said, "I'll look into it," She got up and walked to join Zale who was pacing the quad slowly, occasionally bending down to pick up a discarded Manifesto and adding it to the fistful he'd collected.

Hillary remained on the auditorium steps, numb except for her trembling legs, staring down at the spot where Coach had fallen. His small orange megaphone lay abandoned nearby. She picked it up and ran a fingertip over the rim of the horn. Would Coach's voice ever boom out again?

**

Neka Jay returned with Zale alongside her now. "They are going to Dr. Kovar's place."

Zale nodded, and said, "She owns that huge piece of land beyond the valley oaks." He waved his arm. "Inherited it from her husband, Joseph Kovar, pillar of this part of the county, started up the Tea Party in our region."

Neka Jay sat down next to Hillary and handed her a copy of the Manifesto flyer. Hillary could not bring herself to look at it. Zale offered his hand to Hillary. She took it and straightened up, the megaphone still in her hand.

"Let's go to the club meeting room," Zale said, directing his suggestion to Neka Jay and the other students who had stayed huddled on the far side of the steps.

"Can we get in?" asked Hillary.

"I'm not the faculty advisor, but my classes are held in there, so I've got the omni code," said Zale.

Hillary nodded, reached out for the steel handrail and pulled herself up, to follow Zale's lead. As they walked across the bridge over Yokuts Creek, she had a sudden memory flash of a duckling she'd once seen paddling along behind a larger duck, the kind with shiny black feathers and a crested head.

Zale was take-charge and sure of himself, while she was having trouble putting one foot in front of the other. She straightened her shoulders. She had to pull herself together.

The SoJust meeting room seemed almost a sanctuary. The poster on the green "Go" wall that drew Hillary's attention today held no image, just the powerful words of Toni Morrison: "In this country American means white. Everybody else has to hyphenate." Hillary recalled Dean Van Cleese complaining about that, and she thought about the complexity of the issues.

In a voice hard as cold steel, Neka Jay spoke up. "Instead of being arrested on an assault charge, that bearded guy gets to walk away." Suddenly the room practically crackled with energy. "That wouldn't happen for any of us, you know that!"

"And look what he was handing out, did you read it?" cried a Black student with a side-shaved braided Mohawk. "I'm pulling quotes for the *Clarion*. Even if what happened today might not be a hate crime, it borders on it. I heard someone calling Coach a 'race traitor.'" He thrust a copy of the Manifesto at Zale.

"Thank you, Jamal." Zale read parts of the Manifesto out loud.

"'The communism Karl Marx promotes in his *Manifesto* is an idealistic phantasm, out of touch with human nature. This toxic ideology tried to delete the pronoun "I" and replace it with an implacable "we." Communism threw out individuals and replaced them with collectives. The malignant spirit of collectivism flourishes in higher education in California. 'Walk away from Ethnic Studies. Turn around. Become Your Own Best Self'."

Jamal jumped in to echo a phrase, "'Malignant spirit,' my ass. That bearded guy talks like an independent spirit, like some kind of hero standing tall on a hill, but he's a diseased follower of Kovar's, smearing Ethnic Studies."

Neka Jay scowled. "They act like it's free speech, but handing out propaganda is like a hate crime, worse in its own way."

"And now, look what's happened to Coach," said Bayani. He turned to Hillary, his face reminding her of a wizened apple doll, old before his time. "What did the EMTs say?"

Hillary's face flushed, her pulse hard and slow in her jaw. "I couldn't make out what they were saying," she sucked in a deep breath, "but it didn't look good."

Jamal raised a fist. "Coach is our faculty advisor but he's been the victim of hate himself now. We've got this club really rolling." Hillary recognized the fire in his eyes as how she used to feel as a young reporter. He went on, "They don't let us meet without an advisor."

"This is not a formal meeting," said Neka Jay. "But Coach would want us to carry on. We all know that." She looked at the others, who were nodding with glum faces. "We need an interim advisor."

Neka Jay turned to Zale. "Professor Zale, would you be the advisor?" she asked.

Zale pressed his palms together in a *Namaste* gesture. "Let us pray Coach returns soon."

Neka Jay shouted, "But if he doesn't? What then?"

"Thank you, but as a lay preacher in the Episcopal Church," said Zale, "I might be seen as too biased. You know Coach was agnostic and neutral on the religion element."

"Well, I'm Sikh," said Neka Jay, patting her waist, "and carry a dagger under my clothes in the spirit of being ready to fight oppression. East Indian heritage and proud of it." She waved her hand in the air, a steel bracelet dangling against her skin. "Bayani is Muslim and Angel Han is atheist."

Jamal said, "We've got Christian and Jewish. Lorena's friend Robert, he's Nisenan. That doesn't matter, Professor Zale. What matters is you care about us all."

Zale nodded thoughtfully. "Still, I teach African American History." He turned to Hillary. "The WAR class covers four ethnicities and beyond. Would you accept nomination as advisor?"

Hillary's heart raced. She had already accepted William's invitation to this controversial position, a white woman teaching ES 101. "I want to help," she said, thinking of Claire and Keisha and students like them, who needed a safe meeting place. "But we need diverse faculty here to set an example of social justice."

"White people willing and dedicated to doing the hard and uncomfortable work are essential to level the playing field," said Zale. "People like Coach." He paused a beat. "And you."

Hillary wrinkled her nose. "I feel we need to recruit other faculty, work for multicultural leadership. I'll phone around, see if Pamela Fung or Paul Chavez are interested. I think at the faculty party at Little Joe's I heard one of them say they might be."

"You are a woman, though," said Neka Jay, pacing back and forth at the front of the classroom, "plus you are, pardon my saying so," she gave a devilish grin, "getting older, so ageism is entering in, too. You have a little skin in the game, as Warren Buffett might have put it." She pointed to a poster next to the whiteboard, depicting a huge wheel with spokes labeled "PRIVILEGES" at the top and "OPPRESSIONS" at the bottom.

Hillary laughed. What a clever young woman. "Thank you for your confidence! I really don't feel fit for the job though." Hadn't Coach been trying to tell her something about the Club as he lay injured on the auditorium steps? She shook off the thought.

"Think about it over the weekend," said Zale.

She nodded, but she knew she couldn't take on this responsibility. Sure, she was effective in the classroom but not up to the job of keeping tabs on students in such an activist group as this.

**

Hillary and Zale took the footbridge back to the admin building. She paused to watch a trout dart about in the shade under the bridge. The fish was as innocent of today's mayhem as its forebears had been of men with Gold Rush fever who pushed the Nisenan off this land.

When they got to the quad, a half dozen crows strode toward them over the grass, their beaks whisking aside torn paper not yet collected by the grounds keepers, even bits of Nettie's Manifesto.

"That Manifesto," said Zale. "Did you know our colleague Frank Stern published a book he called a manifesto?"

Hillary nodded. "Quite the genre, the manifesto. I've seen Frank's, yes. All about standing alone. Ironically, he and Dr. Kovar seem to be birds of a feather in the same nest."

As Hillary and Zale neared the admin building, the crows cawed one after another in call-and-response, as if warning them. "A murder of crows," said Zale.

Hillary turned to study the black birds. "That word 'murder' came from the Book of Saint Albans, five hundred years ago," she said. "It was about hunting, not that different from what we see here. Hunting and death. If we open our eyes." Hillary looked into the sky, smoky from wildfires blazing all over Northern California. "Natural and unnatural."

Zale nodded, patting his phone. "Dupree just sent a text. He's convinced the higher-ups that he should keep a closer eye on us."

At Hillary's puzzled expression, Zale went on, "Ever since you reported those dolls." He shook his head and sighed. "Dupree took the hanged figures down and put them into evidence. Doesn't look like anyone else saw them."

"I don't know if I did the right thing to keep my daughter and her friend from that awful sight. Maybe they should have seen it." She looked at Zale. His face was calm, listening. He was a person she could open up to.

"I feel ashamed of what white people have done and how so many of them don't see it." She yanked open the heavy glass door of the admin building. "Or I should say, so many of us. I can't get over the color-blind part. I was that way, myself, until my daughter came out, and I started to look more deeply into my automatic reactions, to let myself notice them, not shove them under so fast."

"Everyone has absorbed racism from the culture and it will always be with us. But it's worthwhile to resist. Essential, even." Zale pressed her: "One good move would be to accept being the interim faculty advisor for the club."

"I can't take that over when they should have someone of color. I'll contact Pablo."

"Pablo?"

Hillary's face flushed. "Paul, I mean Paul." Her heart pounded over what had slipped out of her mouth—Pablo, a stereotypical name for a Hispanic man.

Where had that come from?

18

SATURDAY, AUGUST 28

Hillary had Stacy over, watching the big TV in the basement tuned to 2021's March on Washington, D.C., marking the anniversary of Martin Luther King's "I Have a Dream" speech, calling for an end to racism in the United States. Claire and Keisha were in downtown Sacramento at the Capitol March for Voting Rights.

"I had plenty troubles in my life but no trouble voting, myself," said Stacy. "Trouble getting down your basement steps, yes ma'am."

"You get that knee replacement, and it will make a difference," Hillary said. Stacy had put on some pounds when her knee started to hurt a couple years ago. It worried Hillary that Stacy might become borderline diabetic, but it was Hillary whose lab results showed she was getting close to that edge.

Hillary reminded herself she needed to be more active, get back to karate class or at least do a better job tracking calories on her Apple Watch. Those bear claws she'd served had not been a wise choice. She picked up the last sliced almond off the plate, waved it in the air and said, "Then, you'll march again, and I'll go with you. Make four of us."

Stacy nodded. "I could have gone today, honestly, just didn't feel like it."

"Go where?" called Paisley, coming down the stairs, an iPad tucked under her arm.

"March downtown," said Hillary, turning toward Paisley. "Claire texted she and Keisha ended up on the Capitol steps this morning. Isn't that where you used to protest?"

"Didn't do much good, those sixties 'make love, not war' demonstrations, did they? Organizers just want to steal your time to promote their interests. Better use your energy on your own talent, like artists in the Romantic Era." Paisley thrust her iPad at Hillary. The screen displayed a feature article about the art show Paisley had helped put together. "The show in the campus gallery opens Monday. We made some brilliant selections."

Hillary's pulse raced when her mother discussed art. "Romantics," Hillary said. "Not sure how many people will care about art from the eighteen-hundreds." Her mother had visions of artistic great-ness, abandoning Hillary so long ago to run off to the South Pacific with her art teacher. The truth was, she stole part of Hillary's childhood and even now expected everyone to be fascinated by her aesthetic choices. The hurt smoldered, deep inside Hillary.

"Those marches and demonstrations, they did do some good," argued Stacy. "Don't discount 'em. And voting matters."

"Well, voting doesn't last anyway. The ebb and flow of public opinion." Paisley placed her iPad into Stacy's line of sight. "Now, take a look at this work of genius."

"Were we on TV?" Claire bounded down the stairs followed by Keisha, hand clamped onto the top of her head to keep from knocking it against the low ceiling over the stairs. Darius came loping down last, a hand-drawn sign still hanging from his collar —*I'm not a voter, but I hope you are!*

"Hello to you, too!" Hillary laughed at the distraction the teens and the dog provided, diverting attention from Paisley and her iPad art photos. "We didn't see the state capitol on TV. We had the Washington, D.C. march on."

"We wanted to be on TV," Keisha said, "so if Coach woke up from his coma he could see us on the news. He wanted to be at that march."

"I haven't heard from his wife, so no news is good news," said Hillary.

"You'd be better off out shooting baskets, girls," said Paisley. "Become the most powerful players you can, the heroes of your own life. Take a look at this painting."

She thrust her iPad in front of Claire. "It's a print of Gainsborough's *Blue Boy*. Look at him, a splendid youth, anticipating a heroic future, don't you think?" Paisley's gray eyes sparkled.

Claire looked at the image on the iPad and darted a glance at Keisha, who was giving Stacy a shoulder massage.

Stacy reached up to pat her granddaughter's hand. "Thank you, honey." She leaned forward to grip the arms of her chair. She stood slowly, cleared her throat and spoke. "We need to get a move on, get over to Oak Park for the benefit game, get you both warmed up with your team."

Hillary looked at Paisley. "There's room for all of us in the SUV," she said. "Come along and watch the girls play ball. Help raise money for voters' rights."

"Count me out," said Paisley. "I'll be in the garage, working on my portrait of President Trump." She closed the cover of her iPad, mounted the stairs and vanished.

Hillary took a deep breath. There was her mother, gone again. In more ways than one. Hillary vowed not to abandon Claire and the communities they cared about.

19

MONDAY, AUGUST 30

As she moved about on campus, Hillary couldn't help but look up into the trees. She spotted no repeat of the gruesome tableau from a week ago and released a shaky breath.

Claire and Keisha were on campus for their Early College classes, and Hillary was on her way to their afternoon basketball practice. She was relieved to see the widespread sycamore branches hosting a pair of chattering squirrels chasing through the leafy branches. Nothing more.

She wasn't sure who she would find in the gym. Coach's wife, Phyllis, had phoned from the hospital to let her know of his continuing critical status. His fractured skull had not protected his brain from severe damage. Hillary sensed a huge and hollow shell from his absence on campus.

On the hardwood court inside, she recognized Tiffany Singh, with her long blond hair pulled down into a businesslike ponytail, running the practice. Hillary sat at the end of the first row of bleachers. This was a scrimmage, so both Claire and Keisha were getting to play. Within a few minutes, Tiffany blew her whistle, and the young women ran to the bench for her words to end today's practice.

After the players ran off to shower, Hillary walked over to Tiffany. "Good to see you here subbing in. You heard about what happened, right?"

"Horrible. Crazy times here to cause an accident like that. How's Coach doing?"

"His wife, Phyllis, phoned this morning. He's still comatose and it's not looking good but she," Hillary paused and took a deep breath, "and all of us, really, still have hope."

Tiffany tugged at the whistle hanging next to her ID lanyard, her name printed under her photo. "Feels weird trying to take Coach's place. It's great to see how well your daughter is doing. Keisha, too. They bonded with him right away last week. They showed me three new moves Coach taught them in just two days."

"His being gone leaves a huge hole on campus," Hillary said, thinking of his role advising the student club, as well.

She changed the subject. "Do you want to come with us to the art gallery? My mother's been volunteering there, and she insists I take the girls to see the show that opens today."

Keisha and Claire ran up. "Mom, did you see Tiffany's here? It's like a reunion!" said Claire.

Hillary smiled at their joy seeing each other again. It had been a couple years since Tiffany had coached the two of them on AAU teams up in Sacramento.

"A reunion. Makes me think of what it might be like ... " said Keisha, damp and glowing from the shower, "if we ever find my mother."

A pang of sorrow hit Hillary. The search for Keisha's mother had run into so many dead ends. Excavating that location in the orchard had uncovered a body, and the sheriff had opened an investigation.

Years ago, Stacy filed a missing person report and left her DNA sample. That buried victim wasn't likely to be Tamika. Still the woman was known to have gone off her meds at times, left her baby, Keisha, with Stacy and disappeared for a month at a time.

It was a heartbreak for Stacy that her bipolar daughter would not stay on her meds. Ed was using his old contacts at the sheriff's office to speed up the identification process. It was so hard, this torture of waiting to find out.

**

Hillary led the way across campus to the Clear-water Gallery, where they found a pair of glass doors propped open. Inside, a banner proclaimed the current show: "*CELEBRATING THE ROMANTICS.*"

Paisley rushed over to greet them. "My dears! Please come in and embrace our treasures."

A sign on an easel promoted a future show titled "Through the Lens of Social Justice." Hillary pointed it out and said, "That looks great!"

Paisley frowned. "I'm not involved in that one. Too political. I'll be working on the Frida Kahlo show and then Sisters' Self Portraits." She gestured, directing them to the left. "Look what we have for you today!"

Hillary walked into the main room of the gallery, followed by Claire and Keisha.

Twenty or so reproductions of paintings hung on three solid white walls. Hillary was surprised to see Nettie Kovar there, with Lorena by her side. Gesturing at a canvas in front of her, Nettie was effusing about conveyance of the passionate self.

Lorena nodded agreement and called, "Hi, Professor Broome." She waved toward a copy of a brightly colored painting. "Come look at Goya's *Parasol.*"

Hillary realized that Lorena must not yet know she would not be getting hired for a tutoring job. Hillary gazed at the depiction of a brunette in a bright yellow skirt and blue blouse, with a flower tucked into her neckline, shielded by a young man holding a green parasol over her to protect her from the glaring Spanish sun.

Lorena tilted her chin with pride as if she herself had painted the scene. "See how majestic they look, each in their own role!"

Hillary nodded. Her phone rang and she glanced at the screen. It was Phyllis, Coach's wife. "Excuse me, I need to take this call."

The sobbing coming through the phone was loud enough to catch Claire and Keisha's attention. They clustered around the phone, and Hillary put it on speaker.

"He's … " then silence. They waited, the girls' eyes wide. "The doctors have called me in … " Hillary strained to catch the next words. "to make a decision. I've got to get in touch with his brother." The call dropped.

"What does she mean, Mom?" Claire asked, pursing her lips.

Hillary felt tongue-tied. They had not ever discussed end-of-life decisions. "Well, his wife has to decide if they should keep him on life support or … "

"Or?"

Hillary took a deep breath. "Or let him go."

Claire's jaw dropped open. "Go?"

"Means let him die," said Keisha, in a gravelly voice.

Tears welled in Claire's eyes, and one slipped down her cheek. Hillary reached into her pocket for her handkerchief, but she'd neglected to replace it.

Nettie had been watching Hillary and the girls. "What's the problem?" Nettie called out in a chipper tone.

"Coach might not recover ... " said Hillary.

"Oh, I'm sorry to hear that." Nettie gave a quick frown and went back to a painting on the wall. She began discussing it with Lorena.

A wave of rage swelled up through Hillary's sorrow. It was all the fault of Nettie's Manifesto. The chaos it caused. Yet the woman didn't seem to have a clue, or didn't care, about taking responsibility for the results of her actions.

Claire was stretching her T-shirt sleeve to wipe her eyes. Hillary nodded in the direction of the gallery doors, and said, "Let's get to the bathroom."

As they left, Paisley said, "You certainly didn't stay long."

"I'm sorry. We've just had a shock. Coach is at death's door," Hillary said.

"It won't prolong his life, whether you go or stay," countered Paisley.

Hillary shook her head, aghast, and led the way out of the gallery.

The three of them hurried into the Gender Neutral bathroom. Hillary bent to splash water on her face in the trough basin. As she stood and looked in the mirror, Hillary saw messages scrawled in black on the pale-yellow wall behind them. She couldn't read reverse language but her heart beat unevenly with a sense that this time, she would not be able to protect Claire and Keisha. She turned to face the writing on the wall.

Scrawled in all caps, were racial and homophobic slurs too ghastly to speak aloud. Hillary reached behind her and clutched the edge of the basin to stop her sense of falling as she watched Claire still leaning over the basin. Hillary had never seen such outrageous language. She couldn't protect either of them this time.

Keisha patted her face dry and tossed the paper towel in the bin.

Then she looked in the mirror and saw it. Without even turning to read it, her shoulders sagged. "No. Not here, too?" She drew herself up to her full six feet, three inches, and picked at her short black curls.

Hillary's face flushed and her heart raced. She turned to Keisha and repeated, "No, not here. Not here, Keisha. Not while I'm here. No." What was she saying? The hatred was here. She had said 'No' to it. But words were not enough. Too much and not enough.

Claire grabbed a paper towel and turned to look at the wall, her gray eyes opening wide, the towel pressed against her lips.

What kind of evil was growing right under Hillary's nose? Who would have come here and scrawled that hate on the wall? All this, and Coach was not coming back.

Anger tore through her, fueled every muscle, but there was nobody to take to the mat. No one to kick or to punch. This was that other kind of battle, like WAR in ES 101. Hot rage pulsed through her cells.

She would join forces with the SoJust community. Add her energy. Say "Yes."

PART II

The smallest minority on earth is the individual. Those who deny individual rights cannot claim to be defenders of minorities.

—Ayn Rand

20

TUESDAY, AUGUST 31

Nettie glanced out the window as she stirred chopped walnuts into the dough. Her timing was perfect. Again. After their morning classes, Fury and the others had come back and picked most of the Pink Ladies off from the apple tree closest to the barn dorm.

She smiled as she remembered her beloved Joseph calling the work-study students his "White Crows" after he spotted a white crow in the walnut grove years ago. Unique, he called the bird. Special, he called the students.

He had done the right thing, keeping his Kovar Family Ranch off limits. Let Apple Acres and those other ranchers invite the public in to pick a bagful at a time. Much more important to allow these chosen few to labor in the vast apple and walnut orchards, to build their skills as agricultural entrepreneurs of the future.

With a melon baller, she scooped up the chocolate chip cookie dough, formed it into small balls rowed up neatly on an aluminum baking sheet, and slid the sheet into the oven. She stepped back and took a deep breath. Her chest expanded at the glory of the American way, even though it had been so many years since she escaped her bleak childhood in communist Czechoslovakia.

If only she could convince more young citizens to understand and appreciate their unique way of life. To want to preserve it against encroachments by so-called progressives. She'd do whatever it took to succeed in her mission. Joseph would approve. She blinked fast. Nothing to cry over here.

In a few minutes, her students would wash up outside, step up onto the plank porch and come into the barn kitchen for their break. They would find a sweet reward for their hard work. She set out a pitcher of cold milk.

**

As she whisked the cookie sheet out of the oven and set it on the stovetop, Nettie noticed Fury staring at her oven-mitt-clad hands.

"That's what a real woman does," he said and sent a sideways glance at Lorena. His stomach growled. Nettie could see he was trying to be patient. That was a stretch for him, always. She might need to keep a closer eye on him, watch for signs that his passionate nature might overwhelm his thinking.

Her White Crows gathered around the sawn walnut plank table, all eyes focused on the sheet of golden-brown, plump chocolate chip cookies, loaded with walnuts they'd harvested after machine shakers dropped the nuts onto tarps for gathering.

Nettie had fostered the students' pride in the quality fruits and nuts grown in the great Central Valley, carved out between mountain ranges as if a giant had taken a scoop shovel to the earth.

Over the last year, they'd been earning room and board in the barn dorm by working the acreage. Paying them added to the expense side of the ledger, but Joseph had taught her it was an investment in the future of agriculture in California.

At one time or another, she'd noticed each of them looking at Joseph's map on the wall, depicting California's long green valley and the way it was contained, disciplined.

Just last week, Lorena and Robert stood studying the map's territory, murmuring too softly for Nettie to make out their words. He was using his pistol to tap on a spot by the Mokelumne River. She would have to keep her eye on them. It could lead to trouble when romance entered the dorm setting.

On the other hand, she noticed that Fury hadn't taken up with any girl. Nettie admired his focus on overcoming his setbacks with ambition, work and discipline—her key teachings. His difficult childhood didn't seem much worse than what she'd had to surmount herself, though different of course. He was so reliable supervising the others, older as he was, and a veteran.

Nettie liked to turn up the heat on her students from time to time, test their mettle in various ways. She slid a spatula under the first cookie and tilted it onto Fury's outstretched hand. He tossed the golden disk from one hand to the other like a hot potato, licking his lips, underscoring her faith that Fury was too tough to cry out over such a little thing.

He frowned at the others as they yelped when she served each of them a fresh-from-the-oven cookie, as if he despised their weakness. Nettie wondered if he could trust them with the job they had to do the day after tomorrow. They should have been better seasoned by now, toughened up. Look how well her Manifesto had done its job, channeling so many students away from that anti-American WAR game into her Entrepreneurship program.

She had delegated Fury to supervise the logistics for passing out invitations to the Don Galt speech on Labor Day. The man would explain what anyone's future could hold, if they made the right choices.

Nettie had scheduled Galt to be among those seated on the gazebo when the parade finished up.

With pleasure, she watched Fury bite into his cookie, demolishing it in three bites. He was so decisive on even the smallest actions. The week ahead would be challenging for him. Sometimes he lost his balance when he became zealous. No need to repeat that accident when Coach's wheelchair got tipped over.

As the other students helped themselves to a second cookie, Fury spoke. "Each of you, take a set of invitations and hand them out." He turned to lift a half-inch stack of printouts from the sideboard and set them in front of himself.

He held up a sheet with the printed side facing out and headlined:

THE MORALITY OF CAPITALISM WILL SET YOU FREE.

"Professor Kovar has arranged for a speaker after the parade Monday, over in the town square. It's the Labor Day holiday put on by left wing radicals, you know, the unions."

"We've talked about unions in SoJust meetings. They aren't that bad," countered Lorena, tossing her head so her thick black braid flipped over her shoulder and lay along the front of her blouse.

"Unions make people weak," said Fury. "We

want people to stand their ground, on their own two feet." He set the invitation on top of the others and aligned it with the stack.

Lorena raised her dark eyebrows. "I might join the faculty union with a student membership if I get the tutoring job."

Fury closed his hand into a fist and planted it firmly on top of the stack of papers. "You are free to make your own choices." He stared at Lorena.

"As we all are," said Robert, putting his arm around Lorena's shoulder. She covered his hand with her own.

Fury reached for a second cookie. "So remember, take some invitations and hand them out wherever you see they will do the most good, at school or else-where." He broke his cooled cookie in half, spilling crumbs onto the plank tabletop.

The students finished their break and walked outside to continue picking apples. Through the dorm kitchen window, Nettie watched them pull harvesting knives out of their pockets and open the blade curved like a hook. She had taught them how to place the blade behind the stem of an apple and pull forward to cut the stem quickly.

They were both efficient and gentle getting the fruit into carts and then to the orchard sheds where trucks would later take them to the packing plant Nettie used. After a year of training and supervision, she could trust their skills and hardly ever had to go out into the acreage anymore.

They were a frugal lot, saving their money and spending time with her up at the big house in the evenings, reading from Joseph's library, asking good questions about classic works by Adam Smith and Ben Franklin. Fury was nearly through all the Ayn Rand novels. Nettie knew that regardless of the background he had hinted at, Fury could and would pull himself up by his bootstraps.

Her task was to call forth more of that liberated power in other students, in everyone, really.

Don Galt's Labor Day speech would be useful in that effort.

21

WEDNESDAY, SEPTEMBER 1

On her way to the SoJust meeting, Hillary passed a half dozen black crows strutting over the lawn like they owned the place. They seemed to bob and peck at random, wherever they pleased, as if tattooing the earth. She admired the way they broadcast confidence. Earlier, she had texted Neka Jay and apologized for resisting the call to serve as advisor.

"Sikhs are always forgiving," Neka Jay texted back. Hillary felt her heart full of gratitude for the young woman's strength and generosity.

Encouraged, Hillary texted back her intention to serve as SoJust faculty advisor and asked to be put on the agenda.

As Hillary took the footbridge over Yokuts Creek, she glanced down to look for trout as a good omen. There were none today.

Inside the classroom most desks had been pushed back against the walls, with some left forming a circle in the middle. Hillary was glad to see Zale there. In truth, he was an informal faculty advisor for the group, a sort of mentor or even a spiritual guide for them.

Hillary felt superfluous and yet needed, all at the same time. Zale sat beside Neka Jay and bent toward her, his finger tracing something on a sheet of paper on his desktop.

Hillary turned to notice a young man taping a poster up onto the green wall. It showed an outline of a body, the kind law enforcement officers mark in chalk around a fallen corpse. The rounded shape was drawn in a thick white swath.

Slanted at a diagonal shooting up across the body was a quote in blood red:

Compassion is the sometimes-fatal capacity for feeling what it's like to live inside somebody else's skin. — Frederick Büechner

That was it, Hillary thought. That was the surge that flowed through her yesterday and nearly knocked her over when she saw those awful words scrawled on the pale-yellow bathroom wall. Hillary knew she could never live inside somebody else's skin, but she would do her best to help others in any way she could.

Hillary saw Lorena looking at her, and she took the desk beside the young woman. "I'm surprised to see you here," she said quietly. "The way you left so upset last week."

"I like much of what the club is trying to accomplish," said Lorena, her brows knit into a black V. "Just not everything. I saw you looking at that new poster. Forget about someone else. It's hard enough for me to live inside my own skin, with my family so far away in Mexico."

Hillary nodded, trying to understand this beautiful young woman. An artist and a business major. She seemed like a bird, flying back and forth, intent on finding something. What was she really all about? "Can you find a sense of family here?" she asked Lorena.

Lorena pulled at her braid and threw her shoulders back. "I'm out at the White Crows place, you know, Professor Nettie's. But I'm not sure it's right for me."

Before Hillary could respond, Neka Jay called the meeting to order and announced she was skipping to New Business. "Professor Broome has let me know she's become alarmed at the new hate incidents on campus. One has affected her own young daughter, as well, who comes to campus as part of the Early College program."

She smiled at Hillary, who felt a rush of warmth to her cheeks hearing Neka Jay talk about Claire as part of college life. "So, she reconsidered and has accepted our request to serve as interim faculty advisor."

Zale gave a huge grin and the students applauded politely. Then, the door burst open.

Lavender Van Cleese walked into the room and stood next to Neka Jay. "Request permission to stop this meeting."

Neka Jay nodded but said nothing.

The dean narrowed her eyes and said, "I was just informed by Coach's wife, Phyllis, that he passed away at noon today."

"Oh, no!" students cried out. "I can't believe it!" "That sucks!"

Without waiting for the gasps to die down, Van Cleese continued. "That means your club is suspended until you convince a faculty member to sign on as advisor, going by Policies and Procedures." She stood with pursed lips, her hands clasped at the belt line of her pink shirtdress.

Neka Jay glanced at Hillary. "Professor Broome informed me this morning she would accept the role of interim advisor for us. Will you change that to being the advisor?"

Silence hung in the air. Sorrow flooded Hillary's chest, and she heaved in a deep breath. She exhaled and said, "I cannot fill Coach's shoes, but I'll give it my best shot. Yes."

Van Cleese frowned at Hillary and gave a sharp nod. "Get your paperwork turned in today." She looked at Zale and then back to Hillary. "And make sure your ES 101 doesn't get anyone else stirred up to violence this week."

Hillary stood tall and raised her hands, palms out, in Van Cleese's direction. "Excuse me, but it was Dr. Kovar's flyers that incited the incident. Not the class."

"Well, it would never have happened if it weren't for your class, you know that, and Coach would still be alive." The dean about-faced and left the room.

The students looked at Hillary. Her cheeks flushed with a hot mix of regret and anger, the Irish redhead rising inside her. "The dean seems against us, but she is mistaken. She does not realize where danger lies." Hillary's pulse was racing. How much should she accuse others of provoking violence? Were the dean and her like-minded supporters really going to ruin the class? Couldn't there be room for difference in a peaceful way?

Hillary wanted to steer the various groups

toward a community of respectful diversity. She didn't want to come across as if in a personal battle with the dean. She said, "We can appreciate that from her point of view, the dean is sincere, doing her job, making the system work in the way it has in the past. She doesn't understand we are in new times." Hillary's words were meant to calm the students, but she felt anything but calm. Zale was nodding his head and fiddling with his brass cross.

As if in tune with Hillary's flashing emotions, the lights flickered in the room and the AC cut out.

Neka Jay cleared her throat just as the power came back on. "Okay, so the electricity is struggling again in this old building. Let's move on to our plans for Labor Day before the power deserts us." Neka Jay looked at Bayani. "Go ahead, share your idea."

The slim young man stood. "Labor Day is connected to unions and Social Justice. MLK went to Memphis to support garbage men trying to form a union. Back when I lived in Baltimore, we had a potato sack race at the mosque after the funeral of Freddie Gray. It was called a Peace Fest. It was to get everyone to see that the playing field is not even. You can check it out here on EveryDayAmerican-Muslim." He held up his iPhone and handed the device to Lorena, who took a quick glance before passing it on to Hillary.

Bayani continued, "If you look, you can see it combines a serious message with some fun. That's what we can do after the Labor Day parade when we end up in the town square. And ... " He pulled a burlap sack out of his backpack. "We can modify some of the baggy sacks to show how uneven the playing field is."

He looked around the room at the puzzled expressions. "Like this one." He set his sack down and arranged it with its sewn edge flat to the floor and the sides bunched into a circle.

Jamal shouted, "It's a giant condom." Laughter erupted to break the tension left over from the dean's harsh formality. These students, thought Hillary, so much more savvy than in my day.

"Yes," Bayani said, flashing a thumbs-up. "We can set them out on the ground to look like that. Each player steps into the middle of a collapsed sack. But," he grinned, "ahead of time, we would have resewn some of them, making them different lengths. The long ones let racers hop freely while the short ones make them bend over to hold the sack, slowing them down in the race."

He stepped into the burlap circle on the floor. "So not only is the playing field uneven, but the players' equipment is also uneven, too." He pulled the edges of the sack up as far as they would go, but his hands only reached his knees. "Shows that it's just luck that puts some people into short sacks so they can't hop along on the field as fast as the ones who have full-length sacks." He stood and held his hands up by his chest, his fists curled as if holding the edges of a tall potato sack, flashing his bright smile before he reached down to pick up the edges of his cut-off sack. "The unlucky racers find themselves in sacks that are too short."

"Wow," breathed Neka Jay.

"A brilliant idea," said Zale. The others in the room sat a minute, a couple still gazing at Bayani's iPhone.

"But," Neka Jay was the first to speak up, "it sounds like it takes a lot of time to assemble those sacks, Bayani."

"And a lot of bending over to test it out," said Angel Han. She ran her hands over her belly. "At six months' preggers, I can't help out."

Bayani nodded, his lips pressed together.

"Maybe next year?" Angel suggested.

Neka Jay said, "Yes. What about for now, making posters to carry in the parade and setting back up the booth we used for Orientation Day? Tell people what the club stands for."

"And what we stand against," said Bayani, stuffing his burlap back into his backpack.

"Can we make the signs in the campus art studio, Lorena?" Neka Jay looked at Lorena. "I want to make one welcoming Dolores Huerta's niece, who will speak about the farm workers' union."

Lorena shook her head. "We are not permitted to use that studio for anything except class projects," she replied. "I plan to be with other people on that day, anyway." She stood and left the room.

An awkward silence filled the air. Zale cleared his throat. "You all can come over to our place, make signs in our garage. How about tonight? Say around seven."

"I'll buy the posterboard and markers," said Bayani.

"Sounds like a plan," said Neka Jay. "Let's see what we still need to cover on our agenda."

Hillary realized she indeed would need to give a negative comment to the tutor coordinator. Lorena was not stable enough to work as a tutor, too reactive and unpredictable and prone to lash out.

But Hillary liked the way the other young people were running the club, advancing the causes she cared about. ES 101 was focused on information and writing, she knew, more like talking the walk, but this club was actively walking the walk. Prepared to get into trouble, the "good trouble" she'd heard the late Representative John Lewis advise when he said: "Don't be afraid to make some noise."

Hillary was looking forward to joining in the SoJust's Labor Day activities this coming long weekend. Noise was becoming music to her ears.

22

Thursday, September 2

Hillary was hoping for a productive second meeting of the class. Backstage, she took the sound of voices filling the auditorium as a good sign. Students would have picked up their graded handouts from last week and were probably talking about them or moving into discussing the homework to collect examples of stereotyping.

She paced in a small circle, glancing over her notes from their writings turned in last week. Before they'd seen the Bob Marley video, most students had given greed, lust for power, border disputes, or religion as the reasons for war. A few had written that government taking away freedom was the cause, while several noted psychopaths like Hitler.

Over the past week, she and Zale—green-ink pens in hand—worked their way through the handouts, responding to ideas, support and citation of Marley as a source.

After they heard his lyrics, most students had done well in comparing their initial thoughts to Marley's rhythmic claim that wars will continue as long as the color of skin separates people into first- and second-class citizens.

Hillary thought about the word. *Class.* The word was so like the word "caste," front and center as part of today's topic. So many connections. *Class. Caste. Cast.*

She was concerned over the few students who had scrawled things like "Marley is wrong, skin color has nothing to do with it." Or, "Some people are really better than others." One had printed in huge block letters: "Marley's fucked up." With a sense of hopelessness, Hillary wrote on that paper, "Can you give reasons for your view?"

Would the student with that ID number even be in class today? What good could ES 101 be doing for students like that? Or maybe, what harm?

Zale rushed in through the side door, out of breath. "Sorry to be running late," he said. "Dupree's been keeping a close eye on the campus since you reported those lynched dolls last week. He wanted me to see some photos and let you know about them."

"What kind of photos?"

"Some students are handing out invitations to a

Labor Day speech. Looks like they could be the same people from last week's manifesto uproar."

"Oh, no." Hillary scowled. "Nettie's followers. How is Dupree handling this?"

"He and his partner are staked out in plain clothes. They'll be sticking around for a couple hours."

She swiped her forehead with the back of her hand then reached into the pocket of her blazer for a hair tie. "Let's focus on today. I hear a buzz in the crowd." She tossed her head in the direction of the audience. "Sounds like discussing their homework has prepared them for today's class."

"You know Van Cleese is calling it our dog-and-pony-show." Zale gave a wry grin.

Hillary shook her head. "This is not about promoting ourselves." She fastened her hair into the casual bun she wore for class. "That woman is stuck in a 'We've always done it this way' mindset. She and her friends on the Board resent us shaking up the system."

"Onward, to present the depth and breadth of stereotypes." Zale moved the curtain aside a few inches and peeked into the auditorium. "Looks like a full house today—some online students must have decided to come to campus. A few are bent over this week's handout, writing already."

The tower carillon sounded its musical announcement at the top of the hour, and Hillary nodded at the student working the electrical panel. The ambient lights in the auditorium flickered and went out. Hillary stepped onto the stage.

She looked up at the opening assignment projected on the big screen: **DISCUSS STEREO-TYPES YOU FOUND WITH SOMEONE SITTING NEAR YOU.**

She turned to the audience and pressed her remote clicker. The slide projected above her now read: **ON TODAY'S HANDOUT, WRITE DOWN WHAT COULD BE GOOD ABOUT STEREOTYPES.**

As the lights came back on, Hillary watched many students stare into space, others frown and turn to one another, while some began writing furiously.

At the two-minute mark, Zale strode onto the stage and joined her as she advanced the slide with her clicker. It now pictured the outline of a human head, being hit by an onslaught of tiny images.

Myriad colors and shapes of trees, rocks, birds, clouds, bears, leaves, and fish flashed for split seconds on to the hapless head, before it was attacked by more images, as if the head were under assault by artillery.

At the same time, discordant sounds poured into the air of the auditorium, the volume increasing as the speed of the images quickened to add in cars, stoplights, televisions, stoves, pizzas, knives, guns, and postage stamps.

Without warning, the head imploded on itself to a tiny dot on the screen and disappeared.

Silence filled the space.

Hillary pushed the clicker and **STIMULUS OVERLOAD** appeared on the screen in a giant font.

"Humans are bombarded with trillions of bits of input every second," Zale said.

"We wouldn't be able to deal with the daily onslaught of people and objects if we couldn't predict a lot about them and feel that we know who and what they are," added Hillary.

Zale wrapped his arms about himself in a hug.

"To protect ourselves from being crushed, we invented . . ." She pressed her clicker and in frosty ice-cube letters on the screen, students read **GENERALIZATIONS.**

"We generalize," Hillary said, pointing up at the screen. "We put particulars into categories, we simplify chaos so as to manage our lives and the reality of so much stimuli. That's the business of a college English Department, too: having students practice forming general ideas from the mishmash in their minds and then supporting them with carefully selected specifics."

Hillary pointed up to the screen, showing a quote from Jordan Peterson: "You have an interpretive structure and you couldn't understand anything without it. Your very body is an interpretive structure. It's been crafted over three billion years of evolution. Without that, you wouldn't be able to perceive anything, and it's taken a lot of death and struggle and tragedy to produce you, the thing that's capable of encountering this immense chaos that surrounds us and transforming it into habitable order."

The quote dissolved into a swarming collage of images, then the word **GENERALIZATIONS** came back on the screen, followed quickly by the word **STEREOTYPES**. Hillary shouted out, "What is the difference between a generalization and a stereotype?"

Zale called back at her: "Where did stereotypes come from, anyway?"

A YouTube video filled the screen, showing a cartoon of a sallow-complexioned, thin bald man with white eyebrows and a long white beard. He began speaking about the word "stereotype" as his face dissolved into an image of an old-fashioned printing press bombarded by tiny letters of the alphabet. The letters sorted themselves out on a tray to spell words in lines, then the lines pushed up against each other and were held tightly in a square frame. Ink flowed over them, and a sheet of white paper pressed itself on top. Pouring forth from this odd sandwich was a page from a Gutenberg Bible, magnified large on the screen, its words in an unreadable German font.

The sounds of a ticking clock filled the air as the photo of the Bible morphed into the face of a huge clock with hands moving in slow motion until they stopped.

The sounds of ticking continued as Hillary spoke. "Gutenberg's moveable type printing process took so much time and the loose configuration of the lines came apart after not that many copies were printed," said Hillary. "So a sort of papier-mâché was pressed on top of the frame holding the letters, to make a mold of the page. When the mold was dry, hot metal was poured in to make one piece, a rigid sheet of letters in lines, called a stereotype."

"Stereo," said Zale, "is from the Greek word *stereos, meaning* 'solid.' In those print shops, they called that solid metal sheet a stereotype to contrast it to their original use of moveable type for printing. It is the immovable quality of the plate that we have taken the meaning from, to indicate solidifying anything or any group into a simplified and rigid immovable form."

The word "stereotype" glistened in a metallic font on the screen as Hillary took a turn speaking. "Over the passing of years, the word *stereotype* became a metaphor for any set of ideas repeated identically or with only minor changes."

An image of a single stick figure standing apart from a cluster of figures in a bunch came onto the screen. "As the linguist Deborah Tannen has said, 'We are unique individuals, but we tend to see others as representatives of groups. It's a natural tendency and useful ability to see patterns of similarity.' This human tendency towards creating patterns from chaos that Tannen talks about can lead to stereotyping, some useful, some not so much."

A smiley face burst onto the screen. Hillary called out to the seated students, "Raise your hand if you collected any examples of good stereotypes this past week. What stereotypes did you find that seem positive?"

"No!" came a roar from the back of the auditorium. "No!" A young man jumped up from his aisle seat and ran forward, clutching a stack of papers high in the air. He yelled, "There are no good or bad stereotypes!" He flung the stack into the air, sending papers across the rows of seats. "Come and hear how to live your own life, your glorious individual life that craves freedom to live in you! Don't fit yourself into someone else's mold!"

He dashed out of the auditorium as the pages fluttered down on students who reached up to grab them.

23

SAME DAY

One of the pages drifted onto the stage and settled itself in the footlights near Hillary's feet. She looked at it and then at Zale.

He nodded. "Let's hear what that young man wants to tell us," he said in his baritone that carried so well on Sundays when it was his turn to preach.

She bent to lift the paper, but her hand trembled as she looked over the page. She knew she couldn't read this trash out loud verbatim. She tested out her voice and found it working. "We can see this is an invitation to a speech on Labor Day, after the parade to celebrate workers."

Waving the paper out in the direction of the front of the college, she said, "I will be out in front of the school, marching in the parade across the highway into town and hope to see many of you, as well, to participate in this important holiday."

Zale nodded and carried on. "And now, for today, have you any examples of positive stereotypes?"

Hillary inhaled a belly breath to slow her racing heart. The audience looked back, mirror images of her, wide-eyed and quiet. Was the silence due to the disruption or because they hadn't collected any examples?

"Well," Hillary said, "how about the stereotype of a judge as in 'sober as a judge' that suggests a person with a respectable and trustworthy set of characteristics?"

"Or, television newsreaders, those on local stations, do you see them as dependable, respectable and impartial?" asked Zale.

The room bulged with an oppressive hush.

Slowly, a blond woman rose from her seat. Hillary almost fainted with relief and nodded permission to speak. The young woman straightened her shoulders, ran her hands down over the front of her loose dress, and said, "There can be stereotypes that send out both good and bad meanings," she said. "Like jolly fat people or lazy gluttons who deserve their poor health. There can be more than one in one." She frowned. "And none of them are true about me." She stood tall, her jaw set.

Hillary grimaced at the direction this was going

and was relieved when Zale stepped near the footlights.

"It's true," he said, "there are multiple meanings in stereotypes. And often, we imagine negative words such as 'lazy,' 'criminal,' 'loud,' 'threatening,' and so on. But, stereotypes are simply representations of groups of people that we hold either individually or collectively within a culture."

Hillary ran her fingers through her hair before she got back into the flow of the show and pressed the clicker to advance to the next slide and bring up on the screen the words:

Class.
Caste.
Cast.

She pronounced the three words loudly, three times each.

Those words dissolved. The letters morphed into spelling out the name of the main character in Shakespeare's *Othello* alongside of the image of a broad-shouldered actor. The dark-skinned man was wearing a gray robe that reached to his feet, a green belt and a brown shirt with orange details. His head was turned in the direction of his name on the screen.

"Othello is most often played by a Black actor." Zale strutted around on the stage, one hand on his hip, the other touching his shoulder in imitation of a stereotypical stance of the Moor.

"And we have our current-day actors typecast into roles, as well." Hillary clicked the remote to project onto the screen five images: John Wayne as the Cowboy, Clint Eastwood as the Tough Guy, Tom Cruise as the Hotshot, Drew Barrymore as the Sweetheart, and Morgan Freeman as the Wise Old Teacher.

"These are merely parts to play in movies, but some people are typecast from before birth into rigid roles, cages for life, as we learn from Isabel Wilkerson's book *Caste*. Wilkerson writes that in India, a person's caste can be identified by their name and skin color and probably tone of voice and body postures."

A line-drawn pyramid titled *India* flashed onto the screen, divided into four equally spaced layers, populated from top to bottom by four words, with a fifth appearing outside and below the pyramid:

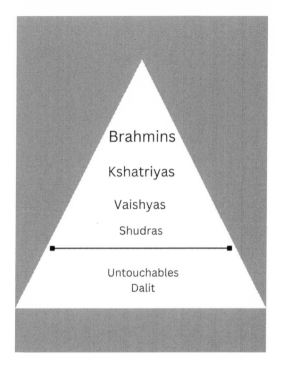

The auditorium was quiet for thirty seconds before that pyramid crumbled and dropped below the screen, out of view.

Hillary called out, "That was a caste system. Here is a class system you first saw last week."

An eight-layer pyramid titled *USA* filled the screen from top to bottom. At the top, like a cross on a church, stood a dollar sign. Inside the layers of various sizes were the terms:

Zale waited a full sixty seconds before he spoke. "WASPS. White Anglo-Saxon Protestants. Look it up if you don't know the term." A giant question mark replaced the USA pyramid. "Given the need to form a more just society, and the human tendency to form generalizations from chaos, how do we create a society driven by conscious stereotypes we like while reducing the types we dislike? This is the million-dollar question."

Hillary continued, "How many layers, how many stereotypes can you see around you in your world? How many are hidden away, invisible, taken for granted?" She reached into her blazer pocket and pulled out a folded handout sheet. She opened it up and waved it in the air. "On the back side of today's handout, write about the one stereotype you see happening most often around you and how that relates to what Isabel Wilkerson notes about identifying people by their name and skin color and probably tone of voice and body postures. Cite what you've just seen from Wilkerson on what you write."

Zale waited a few minutes to let the students finish. "The homework is to write about which of the eight layers in that pyramid you fit into and explain how your background causes you to place yourself there. What is positive about being slotted into that layer and what is negative? What can you do about it?"

Zale and Hillary walked off the stage. She collapsed into the nearest chair, and whispered to Zale, "Did you see Van Cleese out in the audience? She sat there bent over a clipboard, writing God only knows what."

Zale pursed his lips. "And what about those invitations?"

"What about them?"

"Who was that throwing them into the air? Were they only distributed here on campus?"

Hillary stared at him. "Where else?"

"All kinds of places up and down the valley, bars, cafes, gathering spots for enemies of our goals."

"What? How do you know?"

"Don't forget, I'm married to the FBI. Come Sunday to our place. Dupree will serve his barbecued chicken and deliver hot-off-the-tipline details."

More trouble and it was not looking like the good kind. Hillary sighed.

"And," Zale added, "come early to church. It's my turn as a lay preacher to be in the pulpit and preaching for real."

Hillary was eager to hear what he would have to say. How might it relate to what they were preaching in class?

24

SUNDAY, SEPTEMBER 5

On a wooden pew in Lodi Episcopal Church, Hillary sat with Ed for the Sunday service. After the Gospel was read from the Bible, Zale stepped into the pulpit and held up a book by James Cone, a man Hillary had never heard of.

In smooth tones, Zale pronounced the book's title, *The Cross and the Lynching Tree,* twice, very slowly. As she heard that phrase, Hillary's mind morphed it into an expanded image of those little dolls hanging in the tree on campus.

Dazed, Hillary rubbed the Mary medal hanging from her bracelet as Zale continued, still holding the book, its blue-and-yellow cover a background for a sturdy tree trunk spreading up into branches, sprouting a harvest of golden leaves.

Hillary wondered how she never before made the connection between the two upright wooden structures. The connections between Christianity and oppression. So like the hidden connection between American ideals and systemic racism. What ES 101 was trying to convey. Was it an impossible task?

In the hush that enveloped the congregation, Zale set the book down and carried on. "Just last year," he said, "two Black men were found hanging from trees in Southern California within," he paused and held up his hands, palms out, fingers spread wide, "ten days and fifty miles of each other." He closed and opened his fingers four more times. "Now you who have ears, hear me. Police claim those were suicides. But many voices beg to differ."

Anger swelled throughout Hillary's body. How could anyone cover up a lynching by calling it a suicide?

Zale's hands slapped the pulpit. "Our reading today from the Book of Proverbs assures us that 'Whoever sows injustice will reap calamity,' but we look around us to see injustice getting away with murder, time after time. How are we not to explode into savagery at this apparent abandonment by God?"

He stepped down from the pulpit and strode through the middle aisle of the small church. At the other end, he pivoted and stretched out a hand. "On the one hand, we have the suffering Christ hanging from the tree so long ago, and," he raised his other hand, "on the other, we have suffering Black Americans hanging from trees even up until now, in the year of our Lord, 2021."

Spellbound as he preached to the diverse congregation, Hillary clenched her fists. She barely noticed her nails digging into her palms as she listened.

"Jesus, who was both privileged and oppressed, asked God to forgive those who hung him from the cross. How are we, who are both privileged and oppressed, to follow Jesus' example of forgiveness in the face of massive injustice?" His eyes searched the faces turned toward him. Hillary felt a cloak of blessing fall over her shoulders. What a privilege to work with this man.

"Only with God's help. Just like in the baptismal vows: we will with God's help." He strode back up the aisle and stepped into the pulpit. "Give us the courage to follow the Lord's example and pray, 'Father, forgive them, for they know not what they do.' They know not, both the killers and those tasked with policing them. For surely, injustice and cruelty bubble up from the oily depths of ignorance, inside those who do not recognize their own place inside God's beloved community."

Zale's line about ignorance seared Hillary's soul. She could feel her calling thrumming through her blood—the call to educate, to uncover buried shame and guilt, take responsibility for it, not to punish people for the past but to make amends and move beyond it. She believed it was possible even though she knew Zale in his heart felt differently.

Out in front, after the service, Ed shook Zale's hand. "Got to keep a close eye on us law enforcement types."

Zale fingered the small brass cross he wore on a chain around his neck and glanced at Hillary before he turned back to Ed. In his deep voice, Zale said, "She and I both have one of the good guys in our house. Dupree's been home cooking all morning, makes him too nervous to be here when I'm preaching. I'll come along when I'm finished here."

In the car, Hillary told Ed she'd never heard Zale preach before. "Not in a formal way though his lectures often sound like a sermon. He's a lay preacher here, not the pastor. Now you'll get a chance to meet his husband, Dupree, the FBI agent."

"What I care about is what they're doing to keep you safe on campus," Ed said, threading his classic Camaro out of the parking lot. "And out past the school to that little Clearwater. I worry about that place, so rural and yet loaded with redneck ranchers."

"I wouldn't call that Nettie Kovar a redneck rancher," Hillary said. "She's European, more sophisticated, yet twisted by being raised under communism. Wish I could carry a sign showing her face, captioned with 'Beware the Pied Piper'."

Ed gave a snort of a laugh. "I hope you don't choose an incendiary sign for the Labor Day parade. You know I'm coming along to watch for danger."

Hillary nodded. "Claire won't carry signs either, said she wants to be free to break out in a rap if the spirit moves. Stacy and I will though." Her voice pitched louder. "She's disgusted that we have to do this all over again, that the Civil Rights Act meant so little, with all the racism out in public now since the MAGA crowd are in full bloom."

She ran her finger through her hair. "And she's worried about the investigation from the digging at that orchard." She stared out at the rows of grapevines bulging with black fruit that would become Lodi's renowned red wine.

"Okay, just try and relax for a few hours. Have a glass of Lodi Zin at Zale's. Take a look out your window, Chickadee."

"Ed, I asked you not to use that nickname anymore."

"Oops, sorry, it just slipped out. Going to have to find you a new one."

As they drove past the vineyard where they'd

lived years ago, Hillary counted the rows of vines laden with black clusters, ready for harvest soon. She'd been so uptight since the start of the fall semester, she still hadn't returned to her glass of Zinfandel with dinner.

Maybe she should take up the habit again?

25

SAME DAY

Dupree welcomed them at the front door and offered sweet tea or wine. Hillary and Ed said tea would be fine. With glasses of the sweet cold drink in hand, they followed Dupree out to the tidy yard, dotted with dwarf fruit trees in half–wine barrel planters.

"We planted an English walnut in the ground this year." He nodded in the direction of a slim pale gray trunk. "Got it already grafted onto a black walnut, makes it sturdier."

He stood by the grill and examined his barbe-cued chicken, now a mottled red, layered with charred patches.

"Smells fabulous," Ed said. "What's your secret?"

Dupree picked up a knife, and began cutting

slashes through the thickest parts of the thighs. Then, with a sauce-laden brush, he basted the chicken. "It starts with a rub of vinegar, black and red pepper, salt, butter, a little sage, coriander, basil, onion, and garlic."

"Slow down, man," said Ed. "I caught vinegar, pepper and sage."

Zale joined them. "You've got to listen fast around here. He never really gives away his mother's secret."

Dupree transferred the chicken onto a platter and took the barbecue inside. They gathered around the dining room table, where the chicken was accompanied by individual bowls of hot rice and collard greens, topped with pickled red onions and cherry tomatoes.

"I love this tea," Hillary said and raised her glass in a toast. "Here's to a safe and sane Labor Day tomorrow."

"Sweet tea supposed to bring a sweet day," quipped Zale.

"Save room for dessert," added Dupree. "Cobbler from peaches in our yard."

"So," Ed said, "sorry to shift off of sweet stuff, but can you let us in on security preparations you know of for the parade over in Clearwater's town square?"

Dupree scooted his chair back and pulled out a packet of cedar toothpicks. He stuck one in his mouth and sat silent for a few seconds, looking around the table at the three of them. He lodged the toothpick between two teeth and said, "Ready for my rundown?"

Ed and Hillary nodded.

"As you know, our country has suffered not only from a deadly virus, but from a pandemic of hate."

They watched him, solemn-faced.

"Since the D.C. attack in January, hate groups have adopted new tactics, reorganizing," said Dupree, "decentralizing to take their politics local and grow quietly for a time."

"What about here?" asked Hillary.

"In our north state, call themselves ROs."

"ROs?"

"R. O." Dupree pronounced the individual letters. "Stands for Righteous Order, started by a son of the Confederacy, a man named Robert Owen. So, R. O. The members can be identified by sleeveless tank tops letting them show off their muscles and send dominance vibes in all directions. These tanks also been called 'wife beaters.'"

"Wife beaters?" Hillary looked at her glass of tea, wishing she'd taken Dupree up on his offer of wine.

"Named after a man who beat his wife to death back in the forties. A picture of him wearing a sleeveless white undershirt went out and the 'wife beater' nickname carried on through the years."

"Seen plenty of that kind when I was a deputy,"

groused Ed. "Go on. What should we look for tomorrow?"

"The ROs used to wear typical MAGA red caps but during the attack on the Capitol, they shifted to balaclava."

"Balaclava?" asked Hillary

Dupree ran his hand over his bald head. "The name for knitted head-covers worn in the Crimean War, named after the port of Balaclava," said Dupree. "The ROs wear white ones, knit by their stay-at-home barefoot and pregnant wives, that can be pulled down over their faces."

Ed nodded.

"These guys are against what they call 'state tyrants,' like what Michigan's governor was called. Women and trans men are not allowed to join the Righteous Order; they admit only "biological men" and their oath includes a pledge to impregnate women and make white babies. The part we are most concerned about is that they hang out in bars and cafes in the Central Valley and Sierra foothills doing stuff like supporting residents who want the noose back on Placerville's city logo." He got up and walked around to stand between Zale and Hillary.

In a deeper tone of voice, he said, "But, it's closer to home for you both. A nearby group has targeted your ethnic studies class as a tyrannical force. We suspect they'll show up for the speeches after the parade."

Zale scowled. "A tyrannical force? Who said that?"

Ed leaned forward, just as his phone buzzed from his hip pocket. He checked the sender and said, "It's Walt. He's been working the apple orchard case."

"Can you let us in on it?" asked Dupree.

Ed set his phone on the dining room table. "Go ahead, buddy, I've got you on speaker."

"My contact reported that the body at Apple Acres was an African American female, deceased around thirteen to fourteen years ago, with a synthetic-blend rope around her neck, tangled in a gold chain. Cause of death: strangulation."

Hillary stifled a gasp, hearing the news.

"The rope was nearly gone, would never have been discoverable by that dog if it was common hemp, but this was a synthetic blend."

Ed nodded. "Right. Anything else?"

"They're working to establish identity, nothing certain yet."

"Thanks, buddy, let me know when you hear."

"Holy Mary," whispered Hillary, a deep frown drawing her mouth down. Stacy's name was on the report taken when they told the Apple Acres manager what Darius had uncovered. Had Stacy been contacted about the possibility it could be Tamika?

Hillary felt ill and stood up, signaling Ed that it was time to go.

"Don't forget your signs," said Dupree, leading the way into the garage to look over the array of posters and signs painted by the SoJust students night before last.

Hillary chose a two-piece BLM sign to strap onto Darius and hang down his sides and a sign for Stacy that showed the crossing of the Selma Bridge.

Hillary's stomach churned on the drive home. She rubbed her belly and then turned her hands over to examine her palms. She made loose fists and ran her short nails lightly back and forth over where the earlier imprints had been. She had to find out if Stacy knew what was going on in the investigation.

"Let's stop by Stacy's and show her the sign we got for her."

"She'll see it tomorrow."

"Well, I want to touch base with her."

**

"Well, come on in." Stacy held open her screen door. "I'm glad to see you. Our girls are at Underground Books, some kind of launch party for their friend who got her YA novel published."

"We can't stay, but I wanted to show you what we picked out for you to carry in the parade." Hillary placed the sign a few feet from Stacy. It showed an enlarged photo of the Selma march over the Pettus Bridge back in '65. "Do you like it?"

"Honey, it's perfect. Reliving the past. Never thought we'd have to, but now we surely do." Stacy's chin quivered. "Just the way I've been taken back to the past with the news. Did y'all hear?"

"You mean about the remains?"

Stacy nodded four or five times, a whole-body motion. Hillary reached out and held her in a close and quiet hug. Nothing needed to be said.

They knew all they could do was wait for the DNA results.

26

MONDAY, SEPTEMBER 6, LABOR DAY

It was hot in the Central Valley, with the mercury leaping toward a lunch date with the century mark. In Hillary's Forester, the AC was set on max but barely managed to keep the five of them comfortable on the drive down to Clearwater.

Hillary was close to feverish with worry over the speech described in those flyers thrown all over the auditorium last week. She knew the speaker to be an extremist who preached a gospel of unrestrained self-interest. Encasing fear inside a cool facade, she drove into the parking lot.

Tapping the brake pedal, she threaded past people walking in the other direction, towards the front of the college. Most of them clutched signs or hand-painted placards and some carried them aloft already.

"Glad I came along." Ed frowned as he gazed out his window. "Looks like it's a rough crowd."

Hillary slowed to read messages scrawled on cardboard. One poster showed a figure in a pointed white hat, inside of which was written: "CRT is Racist."

"What's 'CRT,' Mom?" Her daughter Claire reached over the seat to poke Hillary's shoulder.

"It stands for Critical Race Theory."

"Is that racist?"

"Absolutely not. It's the study of how racism is built into laws, but of course some people refuse to understand its true meaning and purpose." Hillary blew out a deep breath. "Some people are using it wrong—" She slammed on the brakes and barely avoided hitting a man who darted in front of them, waving a huge STOP BLM TERROR sign.

Stacy said, "Reminds me of the sixties. Now you all gonna see some of what I been through."

"Like what?" asked Keisha.

"Back when Reverend King was at the Selma Bridge, we marched over the Golden Gate, showed we were with them. I was young and at loose ends 'bout that time."

Stacy coughed. "I suspect it'll be safer today, though some faces have on a mighty ugly look over the signs they carry."

"I'm certain the SoJust students made plenty of signs different from these." Hillary pulled into a space at the far edge of the lot. "Let's go find our people."

She stepped out of the Subaru and watched Keisha help Stacy. Ed opened the back door of the SUV and they gathered to get out their things.

Hillary released Darius from his travel crate and snapped on his leash. She pulled the green bottle from the side pocket of her backpack and squeezed some water into the dog's travel bowl.

"Be sure you've got your water with you," she reminded the others as she put her soft-sided bottle back in its pocket. With a carabiner, she fastened on the small orange megaphone she'd kept from when Coach fell on the quad. She gave it a tug to be sure it was secure, but hoped her voice wouldn't need to be heard today.

Hillary hung the little sign showing BLM letters around Darius's neck. "Good boy," she crooned and gave him an energetic scrub over his floppy ears. Then she retrieved her placard picturing LBJ signing the Civil Rights Act of 1964. Under the photo she'd painted *A WORK STILL IN PROGRESS* in all-caps block letters.

She mentally reassured herself over concerns that marching today might endanger her new position at the college. President Williams after all, had recruited her after they worked together on the diversity program at the new community center in Sacramento. But Hillary was untenured at Clearwater College and not sure how far her academic-freedom leash stretched.

Stacy tied a bright purple scarf around her head and reached in for her sign. Ed and Claire and Keisha carried no signs. Ed had made it clear he wanted to simply march along and observe. The girls planned a spontaneous, hands-free rap if the spirit moved them.

As she led the way toward Liberty Road, Hillary spotted Neka Jay as she clipped a Black Lives Matter flag onto a lightweight flagpole and then slid it into a holder Bayani had strapped onto himself.

And there was Zale, waving the dark blue teachers' association flag in her direction. She and her group joined the dozen or so students holding aloft signs they'd made at Zale's house. It looked like they'd used Day-Glo paint on old sheets stapled onto balsa wood.

Hillary shot thumbs-up to Sammi about the rainbow-striped LGBTQIA+ shirt she had on. They were forced into single file when they reached the narrow sidewalk leading onto the bridge over Highway 99, to make way for any vehicular traffic on the bridge. Hillary almost stumbled trying to keep Darius close behind.

She found herself directly behind a young woman carrying a baby in a pouch on her back. The child was yanking the woman's long blond ponytail, making her head bob as she laughed and spun a sign around in all directions. Hillary was horrified to see the sign read "Secure a future for White Children." The woman turned to flash a beaming smile at Hillary.

Stacy slowed her steps and let Keisha, Claire and Ed pass them up before she started a low moaning. Hillary turned to take hold of Stacy's elbow. "You all right?"

With her free hand, Stacy wiped her face with the tail end of her scarf. "Back in the sixties, never saw any like that." She nodded at the blond woman's sign. "We carried a fake coffin with an American flag over it, show our hopes were dead from all our troubles. Didn't much secure a future for us."

Hillary nodded, sick at heart. "Can't give up. Have to keep on marching."

Stacy straightened her shoulders and lifted her sign high. "I'm with you, girl." Hillary had to laugh. In her late forties, she found it energizing to be called "girl," energizing and motivating at the same time, to stay strong.

As she neared the midpoint of the bridge, she gripped Darius's leash close and stepped one foot down onto the street to avoid Lorena, pressed up against the railing. Lorena clutched the top side of a banner and was looking down at Highway 99. Stunned, Hillary recognized who was holding the other end of the long banner: the bearded man who'd knocked Coach over in his wheelchair. She strained to read what was on the banner but couldn't tell what it said.

Below, loud air horn blasts from a semi-truck that was approaching the bridge startled Hillary and Stacy. They stumbled onto the street, causing Darius to bark sharply. Jittery, they stepped back on the sidewalk and inched their way across the bridge until it widened enough to let marchers fan out along both sides of Main Street.

Hillary's spirits lifted at joining back up with Ed, Keisha and Claire. And there were supportive towns-folk, joining in from side streets. Hillary smiled at the sight of a woman with white curls piled into a bunch on top of her head carrying a sign that read:

Climate Justice = Racial Justice.

But Hillary's stomach clenched when she saw a beefy man clutching a shingled board claiming

Ethnic Studies promotes racial preferences

She considered asking him why he thought that, but he disappeared into the growing crowd of bodies passing, oohing and ahhing at the signs from opposing views. It looked to be a testimony to the value of free speech in its own way.

She gave an appreciative nod to a Black woman

carrying a wide sign in the shape of a casket, reading:

Black genocide—1619-2021

And there was Jason, a faculty colleague Hillary recognized as a teachers' union leader, who'd affixed a handmade sign to a yardstick. He was bobbing it up and down and chanting the words aloud:

JESUS HAD TWO DADS,
AND HE TURNED OUT FINE.

Under a wide-brimmed sombrero, a man in tight pants and a short jacket carried a United Farm Workers flag sporting the stylized Aztec black eagle inside a white circle on a red background.

Lorena rushed by, clenched hands spread across the top end of her banner. As Hillary took in the image and read what was printed on it, she felt gooseflesh rise on her arms. She understood that drivers down on 99 had been honking in favor of stenciled outlines of people falling off a cliff, urged on by words that read:

Honk if you want to
Push off BIPOC

"What's BIPOC?" asked Claire.

"Black, indigenous, people of color," said Hillary.

"I told you that, Champ." Keisha punched Claire in the arm.

"Oh, yeah." Claire punched her back.

"Give me a B," called out Keisha, rubbing her arms.

"And give me an I," yelled Claire, pointing to her heart.

Hillary had to hand it to them, so quick to turn a threat into music.

From a side street Frank Stern suddenly broke into her field of vision. He held a small sign that read:

I DON'T BELIEVE IN ANYTHING
I'M JUST HERE FOR THE VIOLENCE

He gave her a Cheshire cat grin and said in a snarky tone, "JK. Joking. Events like this sure do lead to peace, right, Professor Broome?"

Knowing the ironic truth of it for them all, Hillary pointed to a placard carried by a woman a few feet away: "If your beliefs fit on a sign, Think harder."

The marchers sorted themselves into clusters, some darting an evil eye at their opposite numbers. Others looked bland and dispassionate.

She noticed a few in sleeveless white T-shirts

with white knit caps and was chilled to suspect they were members of the Righteous Order. She shot a look at Ed, who gave a sharp nod in return and set his lips into a firm straight line.

With the skill she'd learned as a young reporter, she estimated nearly three hundred people were making their way into Clearwater's Town Square, where an elevated gazebo stood. This was the platform where the Labor Day speakers would deliver their messages. Festooned from the railings of the octagonal structure were three-by-five-foot fans of red, white and blue stripes-and-stars bunting, like scallops on the edges of a wedding cake. The simple white gazebo had been transformed into a patriotic icon.

Off to the side was a bank of flags set up on poles ahead of the event. The American Stars and Stripes stood next to the gazebo, and lined up beside it was a Happy Labor Day flag showing images of a wrench, hard hat and pliers, then a United Farm Workers flag sporting its black eagle on a white circle set into a field of red.

Near those flags, Hillary got Stacy settled in the second row, holding a place for her and Ed. Zale took a seat on one of the chairs set up at the edge of the concrete section facing the gazebo. He planted the pole holding the teachers' union flag in the grass next to him. Just in front of him sat Neka Jay, fiddling with the telescopic aluminum flagpole that held the BLM flag.

Nearby, pop-up canopies had been erected with tables underneath. Jamal and his friends were finishing up getting the Social Justice club booth organized. Hillary led Darius to one of the anchor poles in the back of the pop-up and set her sign aside. She threaded his leash through its loop handle to station him there out of harm's way. She set out his bowl and squirted in water from her green bottle, then went to help Jamal place a stack of *The Clarion* on the tabletop. Beside the newspapers, he set a little sign: "Free College Newspapers."

Hillary admired the way he used clear packing tape to fasten the front page of the paper to the table, so it hung down in full view of the passersby. Even more so, she appreciated the headline he'd written for today's paper, challenging readers with a question:

R U WE or R U I?

But she was alarmed to hear a voice shouting from the crowd in Jamal's direction, "Damn all you crazy Antifa kids!" She couldn't spot who was yelling though.

Ed strolled, taking pictures of the scene, and Hillary saved his place as she joined Stacy in the second row while Claire and Keisha hung out with their friends from the college basketball team.

The eight-piece Clearwater High School marching band blasted out the last few notes of the National Anthem, and Clearwater's mayor took the gazebo steps to the podium, removed his red baseball cap and placed it over his heart to lead the Pledge of Allegiance.

Hillary held her breath for a few seconds, and crossed her fingers before she remembered to breathe with her belly to calm her fears. But the pledge seemed to unite the marchers and they got through to the end without incident.

Mayor Paulson called out a Labor Day welcome from the podium and added, "Proud of our Clearwater Big Red Band for making this a stellar patriotic celebration today. And thanks to the county Central Labor Council setting up this location with the leadership of the United Farm Workers Union. We have a great lineup of speakers for you. Here to present the first one is Professor Nettie Kovar, whom we all love and respect for carrying on the work of our esteemed Joseph and his contributions to our whole region."

Hillary watched Nettie mount the steps, looking like a pale version of Natalie Portman, her black hair short, silky, and straight in a cap cut. More petite than her persona projected, she stood on her tiptoes at the lectern, wiry, strong, and laughing.

Nettie looked elegant, independent, and courageous.

Hillary suppressed a pang of envy as Nettie addressed the crowd, wishing she could be less insecure and more assertive about her convictions, like the woman on the stage.

"Each day here in America, I am grateful as a legal," she stressed the word 'legal,' "yes, a *legal* immigrant. So long ago I escaped my past in communist Czechoslovakia with its mind-numbing gray uniformity. Now, I work to teach the power of individual vision in contrast to a growing tribal collectivism because it takes away personal choice and what all persons have in common and squeezes people into their unchosen legacies and how they are different from other groups. Today, I am pleased to introduce Don Galt, from the Ayn Rand Institute, which offers educational experiences to promote Rand's principles."

There was an expectant silence punctuated by a shout of "America First!" Then a square-jawed man stepped to the podium, thanked Nettie and began to speak. "I am here to support individual labor on Labor Day, personal achievement, productivity, rational self-interest and freedom," he said and launched into what sounded like a canned speech to Hillary. "America has been built into the largest economy in the history of the world as a result of capitalism," he said and went on to describe Adam

Smith's invisible hand of the market and heralding what he called "good greed," contrasting an exemplary Steve Jobs with the failed businessman Bernie Maddow.

Don Galt urged those gathered to love what they did as individuals who work and labor. He finished by quoting from Steve Jobs' address to the Stanford graduating class of 2005: " ... the only thing that kept me going was that I loved what I did ... the only way to do great work is to love what you do."

Galt stepped away from the podium and leaned down over the white railing of the gazebo to touch the top edge of the American flag bunting. "And therefore, on this Labor Day, let me remind you real Americans to keep in your field of vision the supreme value of the individual 'I' acting on your own self-interest to provide the freedom to live your own best life. No need to join a union. No. Lift yourself up by your own bootstraps to reach your dreams."

Adrenaline surged through Hillary's veins at the cheerleading for being self-centered, and a shout rose to her throat, but she held in check her instinct to yell out that he was wrong. She was glad to see the Social Justice Club students stifle what she guessed were their opposing views and stand calmly silent at the rousing applause from one side of those gathered in the park.

Hillary's pulse rate returned to normal as the

mayor introduced Jacquie Fernandez-Lenati, a great-niece of labor leader and civil rights activist Dolores Huerta.

The young woman with long black hair and a brilliant smile stood to say she was there not to give a speech but to just support the Labor Day event and encouraged the audience to "show up" as Hispanic and Latinx citizens. She also urged the community to support other minorities, such as the LGBTQ and African American communities. "When minorities join together, we become the majority," Fernandez-Lenati said. Neka Jay and the other students stood and cheered as she sat.

The mayor announced for the final speaker of the day, Clearwater College President Booker Williams. The handsome college administrator stepped to the podium. "Thank you, Mayor and town leaders, for providing this event on an important day for American workers. To speak to the bootstraps meme Mr. Galt said he so admires, I offer a quote from MLK, Jr., 'It's all right to tell a man to lift himself by his own bootstraps, but it is cruel jest to say to a bootless man that he ought to lift himself by his own bootstraps.'

"Let me start my own talk by moving from boots on the ground to water in the river by responding with a quote from another leader, Bishop Desmond Tutu: 'There comes a point where we need to stop pulling people out of the river. We need to go upstream and find out why they're falling in.'

"And let me ask you gathered here in this park not far from the Mokelumne River, what people have you seen being pulled out of the water? What people have you seen struggling to stay afloat? Who've you noticed wearing life jackets? Who gets pushed naked into the flow? Who is doing the pushing? Did you ever spot any folks who had weights tied to their legs? Their arms? Around their necks? What people have you seen navigating in rafts? How about those stepping into fishing boats? Onto sailboats at the marina?

"I am speaking to the importance of moving beyond the individual cowboy and his bootstraps and his 'I' pronoun and over to learning about some folks who are part of a 'we' pronoun and their footwear of various styles.

"The free individual as trader with other free individuals is indeed to be admired, but the world is not made of all free individuals; it has enslaved individuals, as well. So, I ask you to keep this day in mind and reflect on what you and all of us together can learn from each other on this Labor Day weekend. And what students at Clearwater College can learn from our new ethnic studies program, introduced this fall by Professors Grover Zale and Hillary Broome." He gestured towards them to stand and receive recognition. "And from our student Social Justice Club."

Hillary's heart swelled with gratitude for this man who'd offered her the opportunity to teach ES 101. At the sound of cheers from the crowd, Hillary stood and turned to wave to shouts of "Black Lives Matter" mixed with "Critical Race Theory is communist."

Zale and Neka Jay rose to their feet. Neka Jay stepped forward, lifted her flagpole and waved the BLM flag back and forth high in the air.

From the corner of her eye, Hillary caught a flash of fire.

She gasped as flames sprouted from the corner of Neka Jay's flag.

27

SMALL CAPS Same Day

Incensed by the president's speech, Nettie craved a cigarette but lighting up would cause a tidal wave in this mixed crowd, some so politically correct and intent on controlling others' actions. Pursing her lips, she gazed over in Hillary's direction, and a flash of fire caught her eye. Had someone lit a cigarette? Nettie's jaw dropped as flames licked the edges of a Black Lives Matter flag.

A young woman holding the flagpole ran toward the platform as flames spiraled to the top.

Didn't the girl know to drop it and stomp on it? She must be in a panic. As she swayed with the flagpole clenched in her hands, the BLM flag brushed past the red, white and blue bunting on the gazebo. A blue stripe at the bottom of the scalloped fabric burst into orange flame.

Nettie was shocked. That girl had practically set the American flag on fire with her BLM torch. Now there were shouts all around. "Fire! Run!" People were knocking over chairs and pushing past those still seated.

It was illogical, thought Nettie, panicking like this.

She looked for Fury, spotting him at the far side. He lifted his chin in the direction of two men wearing white undershirts. The men raised their hands, the tips of their index fingertips circled onto their thumbs, before they melted into the crowd. Were they friends of Fury?

Nettie turned to see Hillary jump over the now-empty front row of seats and run toward the flaming flag and bunting, her arm extended. She pointed a green bottle at the engulfed black fabric and squeezed a stream of water onto the flag. It sagged under the weight of the water, burnt cinders falling to the concrete, some bits still on fire. Hillary ran past the young woman and pounded at the burning bunting with some kind of rag.

The young woman dropped the flagpole and hunched over, waving her hands in the air. Grover Zale ran to her.

Shouts of "All Lives Matter" rang from the far edges of the park. Nettie saw a sign in the shape of a casket burst into flame at both ends. People ran out of the square, pushing slower folks to the ground in their hurry.

Hillary jumped up the gazebo steps onto the platform, swirled the charred rag in one hand, and with the other held a megaphone to her lips. "Stop! Don't run from this travesty. Come back! Look at it. It shows we need to grow a climate of respect to our diverse community, to prevent such terrible wars against each other."

Now that the initial panic was over, hackles rose along Nettie's neck. She warmed to voices shouting, "No Critical Race Theory in our schools!" And "CRT is *racist!*" Certainly, overly emotional, yet in her heart she agreed with the shouts, as they continued. "Say no to CRT and hate" and "CRT is evil Marxism!"

Nettie turned to Frank and said, "That girl could have set the American flag on fire."

Hillary kept up her amplified message from the platform. "Come back!" The crowd was nearly gone, their voices fading as they ran out of the town square. Police officers and fire fighters had dashed in and surrounded the now lifeless conflagration.

Hillary descended from the platform, holding the megaphone at her side, and walked past the burnt fabric hanging from the front of the gazebo and lying on the concrete. She confronted Nettie. "That speaker today was wrong. Don't you and Frank realize you promote racism with your selfish individualism?"

"That girl was an individual who nearly burned up the American flag. She was touting belonging to a tribe. She's wrong. It's not racist being in favor of the 'I' pronoun." Nettie raised her chin and looked straight at Hillary.

Frank stood a few inches from Hillary. "That powerful 'I,' yes. We could lose it, if your progressive agenda succeeds, like 'I' was lost in Ayn Rand's *Anthem*." Frank snorted. "Too much 'we this and we that' in ethnic studies mixed in with CRT. Even catering now to people 'preferring 'they and them' for a singular self.' World has gone crazy."

Nettie nodded. "And ethnic studies is part of the problem. People need to take responsibility for their own actions. Your class is turning them into warring mobs."

Hillary's face was flushed red. "I was hired to go to war against racism. If anything, these hateful crimes today just show how much the class is needed."

Lavender Van Cleese rose from her seat and directed her comment to Hillary. "I'm afraid the ethnic studies class may be stirring up more problems than it's solving." She turned to Nettie, as if waiting for agreement.

Nettie nodded. "Yes, people have control over their own lives if they will just accept the tools to take their power. My entrepreneurship program gives control over your life, no matter where you are coming from. Group identity should not drag you down."

"Nor burn up the Stars and Stripes and the freedom they stand for," Frank said.

Hillary took a deep breath. "But this is the kind of good trouble that needs getting into, don't you see that?" She straightened to her full height, pulled back her shoulders and looked down on Nettie.

It annoyed Nettie to see this woman try to win the argument by the sheer bulk of her presence. She squared her shoulders and adopted a calm demeanor. "Your class is unreasonable, illogical and stirs up passions in the community. You," she turned to Van Cleese, stepped back and spread her hands as if a magician showing off a rabbit in a hat. "You can place this problem on the Board of Regents' agenda, now that it's come to a head like this."

Van Cleese gripped her own elbows, encasing her bosom in a hug, and stood grim-faced, listening as Nettie continued pressing her case. "It's against everything freedom stands for to force students to take that class!"

With her empty water bottle, Hillary pointed in the direction of the incinerated Black Lives Matter flag. "Ethnic Studies 101 did not cause that hate crime." She turned back to Nettie and Frank. "You are supporting racism, both of you."

Frank's bushy black brows dipped to meet each

other over his Roman nose. "Racism is a thing of the past. Look at how America elected Obama!"

Nettie shook her head. "On Labor Day, we should be instilling the values of American freedom. It's your class causing division and hatred, teaching that America was founded to protect slavery. That's just evil."

Van Cleese nodded and pointed at Hillary. "Face it, your class is incendiary. I have decided to place it as an emergency item on the Board agenda for Thursday's meeting. I shall recommend the school make it voluntary or cancel it entirely."

Hillary crushed her water bottle. "The class is not to blame. You can't do that in the middle of the project."

"Watch me," Lavender said. "Clearwater is a private college. We don't have to jump through regulation hoops like the state-run places do."

Nettie ducked her head, feeling a surge of pleasure reminiscent of her college days on the debate team. Her porcelain skin glowed with a fresh infusion of hope as she addressed the dean. "Thank you for doing the right thing, Dean Van Cleese. I need to check in with my students before their trip back to the orchard."

She waved in the direction of Fury and Lorena. Wondering if they knew anything about who set the flag afire, she walked away without a backward glance at Hillary.

**

Glad he finally relented and got himself a burner phone, Nettie called Fury's number and learned where he was. She struck out across the town square as firefighters cleaned up the mess of the torched flag near the platform, and a team of town employees folded and stacked chairs onto rolling racks.

She caught up with Fury standing at the open door of the Kovar Orchards white pickup truck parked on Main Street. He reached in and gripped the steering wheel, about to heft himself into the driver's seat.

Nettie spotted Lorena on the passenger side and waved at her before nodding at the White Crow students calling hello from their perches on the rolled-up tarpaulins in the bed of the pickup.

Nettie placed a hand on Fury's arm and asked, "Did you see who set that flag on fire?"

Fury stepped back down onto the macadam, a vacant look on his face. It crossed Nettie's mind to wonder what that look might be covering up. He shook his head. "Not a clue."

From the truck bed, Barney called out in his midwestern twang, "I think it could have been a couple guys I never saw before."

Against the hot September sun, Nettie squinted

up at Barney, new to the work-study flock this summer.

Fury stood next to Nettie, both looking up at Barney. "What did they look like?" she asked.

"Just anybody, no one special." Barney glanced at Fury, who nodded and added, "Yeah, I'm guessing some guys down from the foothills for some excitement."

"Think they had tats on the neck, looked like letters. R and O." Barney gave his quick nod. "You wouldn't want to mess with them unless you had a reason to." He gave a double nod and stood erect.

"Well, we are not in favor of violence, no. Better to stand up for the use of logic," Nettie said, "as rational persuasion is best to convert people away from their tribal group identities." She narrowed her eyes as she studied Fury's face.

"Right," he said, his eyes bright with enthusiasm. "Convince them one-on-one. They can listen to reason, not like the squirrels we're planning to keep away from our walnut harvest."

He mimed the action of aiming a long gun before he laughed and jumped into the driver's seat to start up the engine. "Got to get back, start laying down the tarps," he called out the open window.

Leaving Nettie standing in his exhaust fumes, he sped off in the Kovar truck full of White Crows and waxed tarpaulins, ready to start prep work for the harvest.

Nettie wasn't certain how much control she had lately over her fledglings. Should she be monitoring them more closely? Certainly, they were on board to help mount a persuasive campaign against ES 101 at the Board meeting. They'd eagerly add that to keeping her orchards free of varmints that stole nuts and burrowed at the base of trees to weaken the root systems.

She could count on each one of them. It was silly to worry.

28

SAME DAY

Hillary's cheeks burned as she rolled her crushed water bottle back and forth between her palms, the crackling sounds loud in her ears. Nettie had won this round, setting about to destroy what Hillary had worked so hard for. Frank and Van Cleese were whispering, no doubt conspiring together. She couldn't stand to be in their company a second longer. She had to go see how Neka Jay was doing.

Soggy ashes and people cleaning up the mess took up the space in front of the gazebo, its white paint now blackened with charred bunting. Dupree stood studying the burnt remnants of the BLM flag and scorched flagpole where Neka Jay had dropped them, while a CSI took photos of the scene.

Hillary went behind the gazebo, her legs

unsteady, to get back to to the SoJust club booth. She found Zale there consoling the students.

An EMT finished up bandaging Neka Jay's right hand with gauze. "You're lucky you weren't holding on to the pole all that long," he said.

Streaks of dried tears lined Neka Jay's cheeks. Hillary bent to caress the young woman's shoulders in a soft hug.

She held out her left hand to let the EMT lightly wrap her fingers with gauze and tell her to get herself in for a follow-up by a doc. "Those burns don't look all that serious. Painful I know, but you let go of the pole in time to prevent a bad burn."

Neka Jay nodded. "Thank you."

She turned to Hillary. "I didn't want to drop it —" she said, a catch in her voice "—the pole got so hot, I had to let go. But, I'm not so bad off. It's Angel who's in trouble."

Hillary looked around but couldn't see Angel. "What happened?"

"She had to hurry off with little Jake, try to keep him calm. She was spotting. She's afraid of losing the baby."

Hillary felt alarmed. "Where is she?"

"Her wife was here early to set up the booth, so their car was parked nearby. She took Angel to the hospital in Sacramento."

Hillary bent to ask Neka Jay, "How will you get home?"

"Bayani's old Toyota." She waved at him. "He's taking me to the hospital now to have my hands looked at. My parents are already there waiting for me. Did you know Bayani means 'hero' in Tagalog? I'm fine. Don't worry about me."

"I am so sorry," Hillary said. She turned to Zale. "What started this uproar?"

He shook his head as Dupree joined them. Hillary asked, "Do you know who lit Neka Jay's flag on fire?"

Dupree frowned, his jaw tight.

"You've got suspicions?"

"Of more concern was that wide sign shaped like a casket, set on fire soon after the flag. A couple guys in the crowd looked like they belong to the ROs. We've got them on our radar."

Hillary had to sit down. *ROs*. Her world was turning, and she felt she was falling. "Why here, today?"

"Since January sixth, they've shifted to small towns, trying to build membership by taking on local causes. Word gets around. You both," Dupree looked at Zale and frowned, "are likely in their sights. They've got a lot of energy aimed against ethnic studies in education. Want a world run by strong white men. Hetero men. Hate women and Blacks, both, and especially gays."

Hillary sat staring at Zale. "You know you fit into

two of those categories," she whispered and turned to Dupree. "You both do."

"Their hate will destroy them," said Neka Jay.

Hillary sat tall, ready for battle. "Not soon, I'm afraid. The chaos sparked by their fires got Nettie Kovar to convince Dean Van Cleese to put ES 101 on the Board agenda. She is going to argue that it's incendiary, that it ignites violence. That it should be cancelled for the safety of the community."

"No!" shouted Neka Jay.

Zale countered, "That is a short-term view. This is not a track meet. I've been expecting something like this and building a counter-argument. Remember what Dr. King said about the arc of the universe."

Hillary sighed. "It's supposed to bend toward justice, yes, but immoral people are dedicated to keeping it flat-out rigid as a diving board. You know that."

"Equity is worth fighting for, even if it never comes to pass," said Zale.

Dupree cleared his throat and said, "Speaking of fighting, I was able to get assigned to keep an eye on both of you."

Hillary's reach toward a more perfect world was slipping out of her hands. "It's that dangerous?" Her world was tilting.

"Mom?"

For a second, she ignored the voice.

"Mom, are you okay?"

Hillary blinked. Claire and Keisha had come into the club booth. She felt her stomach drop. She was not okay, but how could she let Claire see that?

"I'm all right, honey, don't worry about me," she assured Claire.

But her passion to help make it a better world was a hot iron ball burning inside her body.

Ed followed the girls into the crowded space of the club booth. "I got the sheriff alerted," he said, nodding in Dupree's direction. "Still have contacts over there from my years as a deputy."

"Glad to hear it," Dupree said.

Ed turned to Hillary. "I brought the Subaru back from the parking lot. Stacy needed to sit quiet. She's waiting there for us. The fires shook her up. Let's get going. Enough Labor Day labors for one day."

Stacy. In the chaos, Hillary had forgotten about her. How could she have been so thoughtless?

Hillary nodded and turned to Zale. "We've got to save our class."

"We will. We can do it. Be patient. Good things take time. I'll see to it that the students get the booth taken down."

Hillary gave a smile and turned to go, but inside where it didn't show, she was worried sick about all of them.

Ed took the wheel on the way home, while Hillary stared out the passenger window. In the back seat, Keisha was parsing out a few lines about strong people. Claire slapped out a rhythm on her knees, while Stacy hummed along.

When they drove by Great Valley Dojo, Hillary reminded herself to call and make an appointment. She considered asking Neka Jay to add Self Defense to next week's SoJust agenda.

Hillary realized she had been naive. It was time to prepare in more ways than one for the coming battles. Ed would be away, at another security conference. She would not have her rock to lean on.

She had to be stronger than ever.

29

WEDNESDAY, SEPTEMBER 8

Neka Jay had texted an urgent call for an emergency club meeting. Hillary got there early and helped Zale position the desks into a circle, larger than usual at Neka's suggestion. What with her burnt hand bandaged and the middle two fingers of the left hand wrapped as well, Neka Jay could not help move the chairs. "But I can still talk ... and text," she said. "Barely."

As she waited for others to arrive, Hillary twisted the corner of her handkerchief into a point, then into a cloth dagger, aligned with her urge to kill off opposition to the class. By the time the hands on the clock on the wall pointed to three o'clock, she had tied the handkerchief into a white cotton knot. She wrapped her fist around it.

Clearwater faculty and students stood in clusters bemoaning yesterday's uproar in the nearby town square. Nearly twenty people showed up for this meeting. Hillary noted a couple of students she'd seen in the ES 101 auditorium and three faculty members she'd tried to get to come on board: Paul Chavez, Pamela Fung, and Amy Smith. Hillary gave them all a warm smile. She especially welcomed Amy, a history professor who specialized in the study of indigenous Americans and the rise of the twentieth-century American Tea Party.

Neka Jay gaveled the buzzing room into silence and asked them to be seated. She stood, her right arm in a sling, the other hand cupping her bandaged one while she spoke: "Monday's display of barbaric hate calls us to action in response." She pointed to a small poster and read out loud: "Desmond Tutu tells us that 'If you are neutral in situations of injustice, you have chosen the side of the oppressor'."

She raised her bandaged hand up out of the sling. "The flag I carried was burned in a horrific act of disrespect that torched the bunting of the American flag, too. But that was merely a fraction of the devastation so many oppressed people feel, so many places all over the world. My own family left Pakistan looking for a peaceful life here, but that possibility is fading. We have to stand up against injustice in our place and time. Professor Broome has some news that should kick us out of neutral and shift us into high gear." She gestured for Hillary to stand.

Hillary's heart seemed to beat double time in its habitual yearning for perfection, but the ugly reality outpaced it. Each face in the room was riveted on hers. These were her people.

"I'm afraid we are being held responsible for the crimes of others," she said. "Our small step towards justice with the ethnic studies class is being blamed as the cause of chaos in the town square."

The faces took on expressions of dismay and disbelief. She heard cries of "That's impossible!" and "It wasn't our fault!"

Jamal called out, "I saw some man touch Neka Jay's flag with a lighter! You better believe I'm planning to write about it in the next *Clarion* edition."

Hillary was shocked. "Did you record it?"

"It happened too fast for me to catch it with my phone." Cries of "Oh, no!" filled the room.

"Did you tell the police? A witness is still a witness even without a photo."

"I was too busy helping at our booth, but I'm going right after this meeting. Have an appointment in the Public Safety Office. I'm going to tell them it was not our fault."

It took a few seconds for the room to quiet before she continued. "I agree with you, it was not our fault! Yet Dean Van Cleese has called for a special board meeting to address this issue as an emergency. She will argue the class needs to be canceled because it's igniting violence in the community, teaching dangerous ideas, and is like calling 'Fire!' in a crowded theater."

Hillary tossed her cotton knot from one hand to the other, surveying the diverse faculty and students, then stopped to gesture to Zale, seated across the large circle from her. "Professor Zale and I, with the blessing of President Williams, piloted this class as a new path, 180 degrees opposite from Van Cleese's 'we've always done it this way' tradition, the way of bureaucrats in control of systems. She seems to need to cling to the past, as changing demographics have left some conservative-leaning board members open to rhetoric from both sides, vacillating between leaders like President Williams and Professor Kovar,"—Hillary gulped at her audacity in naming the faculty culprit— "leaving the class and all of us in a vulnerable position."

The room fell silent, a recognition of their lack of power.

Zale stood. "We are not alone and this is not a new path." He cleared his throat and his voice took on the raspy tones it did when he was "troubled," as he called it. "In the mid-eighteen hundreds, Clearwater College's founders were pioneering clergymen who stood against slavery and preached racial reconciliation. Their radical vision got buried over the years. We could ask the church's ministry of Racial Justice and Healing to lend us their support."

Neka Jay smiled at Zale. "Yes, but the college is no longer affiliated with a religion. It welcomes those from many or no faiths at all. It is good to have ideals but not useful to be idealistic and perfection-ist, to reach beyond the possible. Who has ideas for something practical we could do in response to the threat to cancel ES 101?"

Angel stood and said, "In Thursday's class, we could get on stage with the professors and encourage the students to show up in person for the board meeting."

Hillary was elated. The club was going to reach for the stars, carry their ideals into action.

"We need not fear taking up arms against the old ways," called out Bayani, to murmurs of agree-ment. "All's fair in love and war, and this is war, you said it yourselves, professors."

Hillary exchanged glances with Zale, and she said, "We didn't mean it in the sense of a literal war, here and now, but *Writing About Racism* has taken on a life of its own. Please keep any actions peaceful."

"Peaceful doesn't get respect," said Robert. "We need a more dramatic expression of our stand. Think about the smoke signals my people used. We could carry in the blue-and-purple Clearwater flag to the board meeting, then, if they cancel ES 101, we set the flag on fire."

"No," shouted Lorena, her first time to speak. "We must stay civilized, not mirror the violence. You think Professor Kovar is against you, but she wants justice through a different pathway."

Hillary couldn't figure out Lorena, so two-faced. What did she really care about?

Angel stood, her hands pressed to her belly, her eyes black slits under dark brows, her voice tight. "Yes. I almost lost my baby over the Labor Day uproar, we must stay calm and patient. Keep drama out of the boardroom." She slowly sat back down as if in pain.

"You could hold a protest march outside the admin building, get media attention, recreate the effect of the burning BLM flag with flashlights but not flames," suggested Jamal. "Or I should say 'we' could. I'm giving up just reporting the news; I'm on board with making it now, too. Paying attention to the power of pronouns. You. We. I. Them. "

"Thank you, Jamal. Pronouns matter. My preferred ones are 'she, her and hers.' How about going beyond a simple protest march and holding a sixties-style teach-in?" called out Sammi, a transgender reentry student Hillary suspected was in her fifties or even sixties. Hillary got excited over hearing the term her father had told her that Paisley participated in when she was young and idealistic. A *teach-in*.

"What's that?" called out a young voice.

"You must have heard of it. It's a nonviolent protest where people sit in on discussions, lectures, and debates about controversial topics in order to raise awareness and encourage people to action."

Several SoJust members were nodding with wide-eyed agreement. "Like a sit-in!" yelled Jamal.

Sammi continued, gesturing with her arms out wide. "They started in the anti-war movement at universities. The first teach-in was on a Michigan campus in 1965 put on by the Students for a Democratic Society. It would help us save ES 101 if we could network with people who have similar objectives." Sammi sat down.

Michigan. Where their governor was nearly kidnapped, thought Hillary. That faraway state sounded like a hotbed of diverse views, not unlike California.

Zale cleared his throat, stood and said, "I invite you to mirror my church's work toward 'Becoming Beloved Community' and focus our action on telling the truth about race and repairing the break from our college's founding principles."

Neka Jay shook her head. "No, I'm sorry Professor, we cannot privilege any one religion. But we could ask the teachers' union and the Farm Workers' union if they would collaborate to highlight the links between the college and ongoing issues in our community. Could I hear a motion from the floor?"

Hillary was thrilled to watch the students form a plan for a hastily organized teach-in, led by Sammi.

They might have a chance to save ES 101 after all, depending on what the opposition might be scheming up next.

30

THURSDAY, SEPTEMBER 9

Something was wrong with the college's air conditioning. It was growing hotter by the minute in Hillary's office, where she was editing slides for this afternoon's class. Zale sat in a chair and advised her on the fine points.

Dupree had stopped by to talk about the security situation in light of the chaotic Labor Day events. Hillary hoped the AC would come back on before the noontime start or the auditorium would be unbearable. They might even have to cancel class.

She stepped away from the desk and turned on the little fan sitting on a bare spot on her bookshelf she'd cleared to make room for it now that fall was staying as roasting as summer. She pulled out her handkerchief and wiped her forehead at the exact moment Dupree lifted the back of his arm and drew it across his forehead. They laughed in unison while Zale sat back, tugged at the lapels of his suit jacket and beamed his inscrutable Buddha-like expression.

"I used to call this heat Indian Summer," said Dupree. "Before I knew it was offensive to Native Americans."

"Me, too," said Hillary.

"As I was saying," Dupree continued to brief them, "small town bars and diners along Highway 99 from Redding to Bakersfield have seen an upsurge in Righteous Order gatherings."

Hillary found herself breathing fast, trying to grasp the seriousness of the situation they faced.

"These men have the intention and the capability to interfere in local events and produce violence. We've taken witness statements. One of them saw an RO holding a lighter to the Black Lives Matter flag on Labor Day."

"Was that Jamal from the college?" she asked. He gave a quick nod. Jamal had succeeded in giving his statement after their meeting.

"Their public relations screw-up in the January assault on the Capitol hasn't had any impact on their activities in our region, in fact they have grown stronger."

Hillary was rigid with worry. What if any ROs infiltrated the auditorium? There was no special security assigned the place. How would class go this afternoon?

As if a flock of Canada geese had changed course and zoomed down upon them, a series of powerful honks blasted from all cell phones in the room.

A disembodied voice called out from the mobile speakers: "ALERT. ALERT. ALERT. Emergency Evacuation Alert. All persons on the Clearwater College campus must evacuate immediately. The college has received a bomb threat. All classes and events are cancelled until further notice. We will notify with this Mobile Alert System when all is clear to return."

As the message repeated, fire alarm sirens outside the building came to life in a piercing urgency of continuous *whoop, whoop, whoop*. Hillary stared at Dupree. "What's going on?"

"I hadn't wanted to alarm you unnecessarily, but the Public Safety office received an odd phone call earlier, and they suspected this threat might be coming. They called me over from the branch office. They're worried it could be something different."

"What? Different?"

Dupree addressed Zale: "The first call they got was no bomb threat but a deep voice labeling you as a religious zealot, a 'tyrant,' and complaining you are using ES 101 to form a cult, to lead a 'replacement' team."

Zale stared at Dupree. "A tyrant, me? What do you mean, the 'first call'?"

"Another call accused Hillary of being a 'sellout.'"

A fire alarm bell in the hall started clanging. Zale jumped up so fast his chair fell back onto the floor with a crash.

Dupree turned to the door. "Come on, let's get you both out of here. Now." Dupree hustled them down the stairs before Hillary had time to gather her things or lock her office door.

They rushed onto the quad, joining others running toward the parking lot. As they reached the Public Safety building, Dupree said, "You two go on home. I'll keep you updated."

"Will we be able to get back on campus for the noon start of class?" Hillary asked.

"Don't count on it." Dupree turned toward the Public Safety building.

Hillary grabbed Zale's arm. "Wait here, I have to go back and get my things."

"No, we need to leave now," Zale said. A continuous *whoop whoop* poured from the outdoor loudspeakers along the pathway. "Let's take our separate cars. Meet me at our house, it's closer than if you go all the way home to Sacramento."

"It will just take a minute." Hillary ran in the direction of her office, calling over her shoulder. "I have to have my driver's license and I can't afford to lose my work. Even if we have to skip class today, we can use my laptop slides next week."

"Hurry like the devil's behind you," thundered Zale while Dupree stood frowning at her.

Hillary yanked open the admin building door. Those slides were her best yet, perfect, and she had to save them.

She rushed up the stairs and nearly lost her footing on the landing. Frank Stern was coming out of her office, closing the door behind himself. He hesitated, then recovered. "Oh, there you are!" he said. "I wanted to make sure you heard the alert, weren't so engrossed in your reggae music that you couldn't hear the sirens."

What was *that* man doing in her office? He didn't care about saving others.

He strode past her. "Come on, you're headed the wrong way. We have to leave." He ran down the stairs as if the whole building was on fire.

Why was he in her office? Hesitant, she turned the knob and pushed open the door. Propped on top of her closed laptop stood a book with pages fanned open to keep it upright. The back cover was facing her, showing Frank's headshot, a blurb detailing the book and a barcode at the bottom right. It was his new book, *Stand up for Your Self: a Manifesto for Today*.

She circled around the desk to find Frank's business card propped against the front of the book. Scrawled on the back was: "Why not quote a white man once in a while?"

Frank was revealing his true colors before her

eyes. She shuddered at the thought of his being in her office for even that short time.

With her laptop now in her tote, she made sure to lock the door behind her and hurried along to the rhythm of the *whoop, whoop, whoop* from the outdoor loudspeakers.

31

SAME DAY

Hillary dashed out to her car and drove to Zale and Dupree's house in Lodi. She'd been there before, for the reception after their wedding in Zale's church a couple years ago and that barbecue last week. But she hadn't realized until now that this was the street where that psychic lived. What was her name?

Hillary was surprised Zale's car wasn't out front of his house since he'd had that head start on her. She parked and got her tote from the back seat, prepared to keep working on her slides for today's noon class. It would be good to sit next to Zale and get his immediate feedback on content. At least the AC would be working at his house. She rang the doorbell and turned to study the single-story houses on the street, painted various shades of white, each with a perfectly mowed front lawn and trimmed hedges.

When no one answered, Hillary pressed the doorbell again. They were a lucky couple, for sure, settled into this tidy neighborhood.

She couldn't hear anything from inside and walked down the long narrow driveway to the side door in back. The AC was sitting perfectly quiet, she noted, with a frown.

She knocked three times, and waited. Nothing. She looked down the driveway. There was that single car garage Zale was always complaining about. Not enough room for even one car, yet with a room in the back that Dupree used for his office while Zale's was in the spare bedroom in the house. She walked to the side door of the garage and knocked. Waited and knocked again. What could have happened?

Hillary phoned Dupree. "I'm at your place, but Zale's not here. I don't see his car out front and no answer to the doorbell or to knocking."

Dupree said maybe Zale had had trouble with that old Mazda, but he should have phoned. "We're busy here with the threat. I've called in backup to check out the campus, and I'll send someone to see if he's stuck out in the parking lot. You could go wait for him in the coffee shop down the street."

Hillary drove down the street and felt an urge to pull over in front of that psychic's house. Did the woman still live there? She stared at the porch light fixture, shaped like a candle. Looked the same as back then. What was her name?

Suddenly the door opened and out she walked, still a short, sturdy woman, but her long black hair was now stark white and piled high on her head in a fountain of curls.

"Hello!" she called and shuffled down a pea gravel pathway over to Hillary's car. She made a circling motion with her index finger, and Hillary lowered the passenger side window. "You look lost. I'm Caty. Are you my ten o'clock appointment?"

Dumbfounded, Hillary wondered how the woman knew anyone was out in front of her house. It was just nine-thirty. Did she sit by the window and watch? She called out, "No. No, I'm not lost. Just on my way to the coffee shop." She gunned her engine and pointed with her index finger as if the woman might not know where her neighborhood coffee shop was.

"Ah, the coffee shop." Under her bland surface, the woman seemed to emit rays of invisible power. "You will not go there. Instead you face a pair of pathways. You will choose the perfect one because of your core strength."

She closed her eyes and reached up to pick at her curls. "But it may cost you your life."

Hillary tried to swallow but her throat was dry. "I hope you are wrong," she croaked.

The woman opened her eyes and smiled. "Please feel free to come see me, if I may be of use." She turned and danced lightly over the gravel back to the front door she'd left open, just as an orange cat dashed into the house ahead of her.

The woman seemed enlivened to have served up danger to Hillary. She was not a real psychic, Hillary reminded herself. She knew from interviewing the woman years ago. There was no such thing as a real psychic. Hillary had never believed in them. And certainly did not want to start now.

Her engine idling in neutral, Hillary stared at Caty's closed door for long seconds.

A sudden buzz from her phone yanked Hillary back to the present. It was Dupree. "We located his car in the parking lot. Undisturbed. Locked. No sign of him. The Sheriff is sending a deputy over to our house, and he wants you back here. Now."

Hillary threw the car into drive and sped as fast as she could away from Caty's house and her prediction.

32

SAME DAY

Back at the college, Hillary was relieved to see the admin parking lot was nearly empty. Most had escaped from what might turn out to be a bomb. Zale's old Mazda stuck out like an elephant in a petunia patch. Yellow crime scene tape marked off a wide perimeter around the car.

It couldn't be that dangerous or Dupree would not have sent her back to campus. Her belly full of fear, she rushed into the Public Safety building. Ignoring the officer at the front desk, she strode down the open space of cubicles to the end and opened a door into a small conference room.

Dupree waved her in as he paced the back of the room, his jaw working his ever-present wad of gum while at the same time his eyes were locked on a man at the front.

Hillary stepped into the midst of a half dozen law enforcement officers, her heart racing. A short, slim man stood in front of a touchscreen monitor on the wall. He pointed to a map of Michigan displayed on the screen as he spoke to the personnel in the crowded room.

"As you know, schools in many places have received phoned-in bomb threats such as Clear-water got this morning. Yours accused Professor Zale of being a Black tyrant pushing Critical Race Theory onto innocent students, a taskmaster who deserves destruction in the cause of righteousness. He used the term 'tyrant'."

Hillary gasped. The threat was that specific?

She shot a glance at Dupree. He stood silent, his jaw in motion while the little man in front carried on with his arm outstretched, pointing to the Michigan state capital. "These callers are serious. One phoned a college here claiming a connection with a neo-Nazi cell. Another said he was affiliated with that group who tried to kidnap the Michigan governor, called her a 'tyrant' for mandating COVID pandemic measures."

"A tyrant," he repeated and let the word hang in the room for a few beats. "Now that Professor Zale is missing, we must consider the possibility of kidnapping."

Kidnapping? Hillary wondered if instead it could have been Neka Jay or another student having trouble getting out of the lot. Maybe Zale had helped her. Hillary couldn't stand it. She started whispering to a campus officer standing next to her: "Isn't it too early to know if the phone threat was really related to Zale's disappearance?"

A tall woman with thick, well-muscled arms patted Hillary's shoulder and gestured at an empty chair. Hillary turned to Dupree who shook his head, frowning at her.

The slim man ignored her side talk. "This," he pointed to Michigan again, "is where the modern militia movement was born and it spawned a number of known groups, but that kidnap plot was hatched by suspects the bureau had never heard of."

Hillary watched, her stomach tightening. This man kept talking about the plot to kidnap that Michigan governor, what was her name?

The man tapped the screen and it switched back to show the entire United States before he reached to poke at the center of California. "Here," he nodded at the map of the drooping, L-shaped state, "you have the highest number of general hate groups in the country. They have multiplied during the past year. From Redding in the north to Orange County in the south, you are home to nine Proud Boys chapters." He stared at the sheriff's deputies and campus police in the room. "More than any other state in the union. And Righteous Order groups are growing here, as well. Call themselves the ROs."

A heavy dread flowed through Hillary's veins.

An iron-jawed man of large proportions in the uniform of the campus police asked, "So, Agent Javid, which of the groups are you suspecting of taking the professor?" Finally, she knew the name of the diminutive man in front of the room.

Hillary stood and called out, "Why are you so certain he's been kidnapped? There was chaos in the parking lot. Professor Zale could have run into someone he knew, maybe students who were panicked over the orders to close the campus, or the students had some emergency. Zale could have ridden off in their car to help out."

Before Javid could answer, another sound filled the room. It was Dupree with a loud rumble, clearing his throat. Then he blew a bubble with his pink gum. The room fell silent as they watched it expand, headed for bursting.

He sucked the bubble back into his mouth with a popping sound and shook his head. "He would have phoned."

Dupree put his hand on Hillary's shoulder and said softly, "But we found his phone underneath a car parked near his."

The room seemed to spin slowly. She gripped the top edge of the chair in front of her to keep her balance. It was real.

Zale had actually been kidnapped.

With a thud, Dupree sat, his head cradled in his palms.

"I know. I know." She bent near him. "We'll find him. We will find him."

She had to show she could fight and succeed. Find Zale. Save the class.

33

SAME DAY

Nettie pulled into the parking lot, gratified to see the flock of media cars, television broadcasting vans, TV news trucks and mobile studios even though they took up all the spaces where she generally parked her Mercedes convertible. She liked to keep it near the admin building for the protection assumed by proximity to the nearby Public Safety office.

First she would go look for her students. A few hours ago, Fury told her he was driving the Kovar pickup over to campus with some of the other students. They had finished the work of laying down waxed tarpaulins, preparing for gathering walnuts shaken by machines onto the tarps. They'd also made signs, prepared to face off against the SoJust club protest, if what Lorena told them was true.

Settling for a space next to the CNN van, tricked

out with a disc antenna on top, Nettie parked and pushed the button to raise the Mercedes's canvas top, locking it down for security as she usually did here at school.

She got out, piqued to not have a mic thrust into her face for an interview, and saw most of the reporters over by a young woman who looked to be giving a speech. A reporter was using the term "sixties-style teach-in." Nettie had read about the Free Speech Movement and approved of free speech as long as she was able to express her views.

Nettie made straight for her White Crows, picketing with signs left over from Labor Day and new ones for today's agenda item in front of the Clearwater Board of Trustees. That item concerned a topic she knew was hotter than the soaring temperatures in the valley.

There they were, a media shark pushing his microphone into her face while his cameraman had already focused in on her.

"Does a meeting showcasing opposing sides like this one encourage violence?" the shark asked,

"Yes, and we don't need anything more inciting to violence here in our small town," Nettie said, sliding her bangs to one side. "However, I'm grateful to Dean Van Cleese calling this meeting and showing she cares about the safety of each individual, be they student, staff or faculty, so that we can get back to normal."

"Why are you against ethnic studies?" yelled the CNN reporter, a pale man with John Lennon glasses.

"That kind of study is something anyone can look into, if curiosity leads. No need to force it down student throats."

The man continued, "Some claim you are racist. How do you respond to that charge?"

"I am color blind. Each person rises or falls according to their individual efforts." Nettie placed her empty cigarette holder between her lips and angled her head to give photographers her favorite shot of herself, which often led to a comparison to the late, great Ayn Rand. She lifted her chin a moment longer, then pivoted and with a twirl of her short skirt, she strode over to the teach-in.

Her heart warmed as she recognized Larry, a hefty red-bearded man who'd driven down from Red Bluff, loyal still to Joseph. In his fist, Larry clutched a stick supporting a poster board showing Uncle Sam, the red, white and blue figure pointing his finger at "you." The sign read STOP SHREDDING OUR CONSTITUTION.

The man bowed in Nettie's direction. She inhaled deeply, priding herself on being a sort of Tea Party leader in absentia, carrying the legacy of her beloved Joseph. Now that Hillary and Zale had confronted her with their abominable class, it was forcing her to take a more active stand than ever in battling against courses like ES 101. She felt herself growing into a strong leadership role.

Nettie stood for a minute, observing her Crows, under Fury's supervision. She was concerned to see a frown on Fury's face as he watched Robert take a seat next to Lorena.

And where was Barney? She spotted him getting a bottle of water from a table set up by the SoJust club. They did all seem to be staying calm and orderly now, during a speech by that Indian girl.

Nettie thought her name was Neka something or other, too close to Nettie's own name for comfort. The girl was expounding the value of learning about many ethnicities and cultures. She outlined her appreciation for ES 101 to include Sikhs, her people, and asked how many here knew of the five items they were commanded to wear at all times.

At the end of each of Neka's sentences, seven of Nettie's Crows stood and silently thrust their one-syllable signs in her direction toward the TV cameras aimed their way.

YOU ARE AN IN DI VID UAL

Overall, even though they were not yet as perfect as she'd like, she was proud of her students, so civilized, letting the signs speak for them instead of shouting out to interrupt that Indian girl. Poor thing, she thought she was merely part of a group, needed to be enlightened to the glory of her heroic self and her own potential. Nettie made a note to work with the young woman, steer her into the Entrepreneurship program. She had that special aura of success about her, just needed to be redirected.

Nettie was impressed to see two women wearing white sleeveless T-shirts stretched tight across their pregnant bellies and bookended by men carrying signs proclaiming "ES 101 turns Clearwater to Ditch-water" and "ES 101 turns Clearwater to Wastewater."

Nettie felt proud about how her side of the demonstration was going. She went into the admin building and strode along the crowded hallway and into the boardroom.

She bent to print her name on the sign-up sheet under the faculty section of the public comments list, unhappy but not surprised to see Hillary Broome's name already there. On the community comments section were a couple of names Nettie did not immediately recognize. She hoped at least one of them would support her side of the issue.

The boardroom was small, with just three rows of seats to accommodate observers and those who wanted to speak to the Board. Nettie was gratified that Frank had saved her a place next to him in the front row. President Williams and Dean Van Cleese sat at a small table off to the side of the Board of Regents. They chatted in groups of two and three behind the long table cloaked with a blue-and-purple pinstriped cloth and topped with a row of brass nameplates.

Every board member sported some shade of gray hair, as if standing for the institutional wisdom in the ruling body, and punctuated by the tight white permanent curls of Margaret Smith, who'd inherited her board seat as the last living descendant of the original founders of the college.

Nettie waved at the newcomer who'd been voted onto the Board to replace flaky old John Denver Collins, a hippie who'd beat the drum for every New-Age idea that had come along and earned himself a long-standing chairmanship of the board by virtue of seniority. Nettie was grateful the old man had finally relinquished his grip on life last spring, but by then, it had been too late to stop the outlandish ES 101 pilot project that had passed by a simple five to four majority.

Over the years, her darling Joseph had groomed up-and-coming developers and their attorneys to fill vacancies on the board and at last she'd been able to attract Justin Bierce, Esquire, who billed himself as an Environmental Lawyer on the side of freedom and enterprise for California developers, so burdened by heavy regulation. With Maggie and Nettie's support, Bierce was voted on to the Board at the end of spring semester.

Tonight was Bierce's first meeting as a member of the Board. Now the college could return to focusing on the individual student and his freedom, Nettie thought.

She turned to survey the audience. There was Hillary Broome, with some man Nettie had never seen before, a big Black man with a bald head. He sat looking like the wrath of God, if God had a chewing gum habit. Where was Hillary's co-conspirator, Zale?

Nettie caught Hillary's eye and sent her a smile but received a frown in response. The woman must have arrived early. There seemed to be several other people with her, a couple of teens and that old woman with bluish-white hair Nettie had met a few weeks ago at that faculty event. She recognized her as hostessing that art gallery opening, as well. A good, solid independent artist. What was her name?

In the row behind Hillary sat some of those faculty calling themselves progressives like Pamela Fung and Paul Gonzales. So misguided, ignorant of the dangers of socialism.

The room was stifling hot and humming with excited voices.

John McMartin, voted Chairman of the Board upon John Denver Collins' death, twice gaveled the room to order before the board members got themselves quieted down.

Chairman McMartin began to speak. "On this roasting Indian summer evening, our ancient AC system is barely managing to make the room temperature tolerable, so we will move right into our agenda," he waved a single sheet in the air, "which features the item of urgency brought to me by Dean Van Cleese, followed by comments from faculty and community members."

He looked at Van Cleese, seated next to President Williams. "Go ahead and describe the situation that led to your request for this special meeting."

President Williams scowled as Van Cleese stood and began speaking, her tone clear and firm. "Due to the uproar in our community after the speech of our president on Labor Day caused a near riot," she glanced down at Williams who had scooted his chair back and was looking up at her and shaking his head, "it seems prudent for the esteemed Clear-water College Regents to reconsider President Williams' mandatory pilot project, Ethnic Studies 101 and its pattern of fomenting hate and causing violence. This chaos on the campus has now spread all the way out into the larger community as well."

She turned, looked directly at Hillary and swirled her hands like a whirlwind before she turned back to face the Board. "You should consider several courses of action. For one, allowing students to drop what they never signed up for, with no impact on their transcripts. For another, cancelling the pilot project altogether as an unnecessary attempt to parallel the state colleges' outrageous new graduation requirement. We are private and should emphasize this advantage. Finally, you may want to create a task force to further study the issues involved and present a more reasonable set of options." She marched back to her place and sat down, her lips set in a solid straight line.

The room buzzed with comments. McMartin gaveled until quiet was restored before he nodded and said, "Due to the emergency nature of this meeting, there was no time for written comments prior to this evening. We assume President Williams holds to his remarks made publicly at the Labor Day event in town. Is that correct, President Williams?"

Booker Williams stood. "I stand by my praise of Ethnic Studies 101 and the long-term good it will bring." He sat down.

McMartin nodded, grim-faced, and said, "Therefore, we will now take comments from the sign-up list, first from the faculty, followed by community members who wish to speak to this situation."

Nettie walked the few steps from the front row and faced the board. She looked each board member in the eye as she talked. "As a professor of Entrepreneurship, and advocate of freedom for individuals, I am proud to teach here at this private college, not subject to regulations imposed on public universities run by politicians.

"We nevertheless have a Board of Regents made of human beings, subject to political pressures leading to mistaken decisions at times, and I do understand that common frailty of human nature." She stopped in front of the newest board member but before she could go on, a voice shouted from the audience.

"Objection, Mr. Chairman." Nettie turned and was appalled to see she was being interrupted by the big Black man next to Hillary. "This woman is not commenting but rather giving a speech."

"*Robert's Rules*," responded McMartin as he patted a slim book in front of him, "of parliamentary procedure note that comments may include a speech limited to ten minutes and are perfectly fine as part of discussion. You, however, are out of order and will be asked to leave if you continue." He turned to Nettie. "Please go on, Dr. Kovar."

Nettie turned back to Justin Bierce. "As a newcomer to our Board, you may wonder why the class in question was ever approved even as a pilot project, yes?" She was pleased to see Bierce, square-jawed and calm, dip his head in the affirmative, not a hair falling out of place from his silver coiffure.

"Our Board," she gestured at the spread of members seated at the long table, "was pressured by public opinion, spearheaded by former Chairman Collins' influence, to hire Booker Williams as president two years ago, in the name of the current craze of building diversity to increase student population."

She smoothed her long bangs across her forehead and off to the side. "More than a craze, actually, it was a mirroring of the mob mentality running the state legislators in Sacramento, resulting in Assembly Bill 1460, forcing Cal State students to pass a three-unit ethnic studies class before they can be granted their diplomas, despite four years of hard work on their part. Our board then passed five to four the pilot project called ES 101 in a misguided attempt to stay competitive with the public university system."

Nettie formed a momentary moue before she continued. "None of this creating new classes in emotional reaction to a few unfortunate incidents far off in other parts of the country bears up under rational assessment of the situation. Let us consider the classic work by Adam Smith in his *Wealth of Nations*, for example." Nettie turned to smile at those seated in the audience as she waited a beat for her message to sink in before she turned back to face the board.

"Our nation, and our college as well, will prosper by supporting individuals who choose to study subjects bearing on their own self-interest in a free market without government regulations. Indeed, prosper far more than if laws like AB 1460 and classes like ES 101 are stuffed down their throats. We need more individuals of action, such as I nurture in my entrepreneurship program out on my walnut orchards and invite, rather than force, students into."

Nettie waved her arm in the direction of Van Cleese. "I applaud Dean Van Cleese as a conservative civil servant in the best sense of the term, holding fast to tradition as the way to continue the trajectory of implementation of the American ideal of free choice."

She turned back to face the row of board members. "I urge you to keep in mind that Clearwater was founded as a private institution of higher learning and that it is in your power to cancel this class or at the very least, to stop forcing it upon our students."

She looked over at Hillary. "I cede my remaining time to my colleague, Professor Broome and ask if her comrade, Professor Zale, has abandoned her."

34

SAME DAY

As Nettie pivoted and stepped toward her seat, the groaning of the AC came to a stop. The room was still as death. The board members turned to each other, bug-eyed. Chairman McMartin pursed his lips and frowned.

A man in overalls burst into the boardroom, a wrench in hand and a streak of oil across his sweaty forehead. "Sorry, governors, thought we could fix the problem without a hitch, keep her running, but she quit on us. It's only going to take five minutes."

Chairman McMartin scowled. "This is highly irregular." He snapped his monogrammed handkerchief in the air and drew it across his forehead. "However. I'm calling a ten-minute break." He tapped his gavel once against the round sound block.

Paisley, Claire and Keisha headed for the SoJust pop-up booth to get water. Hillary was thirsty but needed connection with Ed more than she needed water. She took off her navy blue blazer, grateful for the lightweight shell she'd worn under the cotton jacket. She walked across the footbridge for some privacy and sat at the far end.

She phoned Ed, and at his "How are you doing," she said, "It's hotter than hell here where I'm in hell, listening to the devil rant against our class."

"I'm sorry about all that. I hear you."

She could visualize him and his tender presence. Tears rushed into her eyes. She needed him by her side, her rock when things got bad. "I wish you weren't away now."

"I know, but I'll be home tomorrow afternoon. Any word on Zale's whereabouts?"

"Not a thing." Hillary wiped her eyes with her wrinkled handkerchief. "How's it going at your conference?"

"Lots of attention on dealing with mass shootings but not much on kidnappings. But I have heard from my contact at the Coroner's office."

Hillary didn't know if she could take any more bad news. "And?"

"That woman from Apple Acres is Keisha's mother."

She felt she was collapsing in the added heat of

this news. Darius had led to finding Keisha's missing mother. "Are they sure?"

"Yes, DNA extracted from one of her molars went through the genome sequencing. The sample from Stacy was a strong match, confirming her identity even so long after death."

Hillary felt stabbed through her heart, like a whole chicken pierced sideways on a skewer. "Who is going to tell Stacy? When? How does that work?"

"It's complicated because it's a suspected homicide, due to the rope and her being buried. The autopsy report would be public record except it might be considered confidential in a pending criminal case. They are running DNA checks on that gold chain she was wearing, try and learn about the killer."

"Holy Mary," Hillary whispered, holding on to the footbridge railing and staring at a huge brown trout sheltering in the shadow of the bridge.

"I'm not sure when Stacy will be notified. I'll let you know what I find out. I'm sorry, really sorry for what Keisha and Stacy will be going through now."

Hillary fingered her Mary medal. "Pray for us all. I'll call you tomorrow." How could she hold it together and testify for ES 101 in light of this awful news?

35

SAME DAY

Hillary stepped up to face the Board, her cheeks red and hot as if she were walking a plank suspended over a volcano. The AC was supposed to be back on but she felt feverish. Was this room turning into an oven or was it just her?

McMartin was saying something: Hillary needed to pay attention. "So where is Professor Zale? He contacted me this morning asking to speak to this topic since he was the one to design the class. Does anyone know?"

The room was heavy with silence, cut by the straining sound of the AC's efforts. Hillary looked at Dupree, who sat stone-faced. She stood, her arms pressed tight against her sides. "He seems to be a missing person; there is an all-out search going on for him now."

A faint roar in her ears as she spoke seemed to help steady her nerves. "The screams of the selfish in the death grip of holding to systems of inequity are howling all about us. Dr. Kovar speaks of free choice yet there is a scarcity of this in the lives of the oppressed, which includes many who are not present to voice their case now, due to lack of transportation, child care and such. Dr. Kovar argues in favor of self-interest, of choosing to hold one's own life as the standard of value, regarding oneself as the primary beneficiary of one's actions."

Hillary studied the set expressions of the board members in front of her. These people did not get it. "I ask you though, how many people have the talent, the education, the family connections, the status to freely choose their lives? How many have bootstraps to pull themselves up by, or even any boots that are equipped with straps?" She gestured to President Williams. "He spoke to that problem on Labor Day, spoke for so many whose voices are never heard."

She turned and gestured in Nettie's direction. "Dr. Kovar has cited Adam Smith and his laissez-faire capitalism as producing the best results for a nation and for our college. Let me point your attention to a student of Adam Smith's, namely John Stuart Mill, who departed from an early belief in the free marketplace and capitalism and came to advise that a mixed economy or even socialism can result in the betterment of society as a whole, not just in the flourishing of the individual. Mill taught that everyone's happiness counts equally.

"Dr. Kovar and her supporters promote individuals pulling themselves up by their bootstraps, yet they refuse to see that many people go barefoot on blistered feet and not by choice. Dr. Kovar and her followers call themselves color blind but what they are is blind to injustice. They are the well-meaning people holding systemic racism in place."

Hillary worried that she was overdoing the blaming, and yet it was all true. "They refuse to face the historical roots of White Supremacy and the orchard of injustice it supports. Even the way this room is organized shows inequality, power relationships, so different from what it would be if we sat in a circle.

"I beg you to leave ES 101 in place to start setting the whole truth out in front of all our students' eyes and ears and minds and hearts."

Trembling, Hillary returned to her seat and looked with pleading eyes at Dupree. "Your turn," she whispered, pulling her handkerchief out and mopping her forehead.

Several board members were fanning themselves with their agenda printouts. Chairman McMartin looked at the signup sheet and announced that Dupree Tyson Jones was next to comment.

"I apologize for my earlier interruption of Dr.

Kovar." He turned to nod at Nettie. "I would not normally be commenting in this sort of situation, but as an FBI agent assigned to the recent disturbances here on campus, I wanted to shed some light on the circumstances. Rather than being caused by President Williams's speech praising ES 101, we have evidence that the fires at the Labor Day event were set by members of the Righteous Order, called ROs, invited to this little town by flyers written by Dr. Kovar and distributed by her students up and down the Central Valley to bars and cafes. This invitation was also posted to online Stormfront events and alternative messaging apps like Telegram and Signal for the purpose of causing this kind of chaos to endanger education about injustice. This outside interference shows the need for classes like ES 101, rather than the need to cancel them. We can't let the terrorists win."

He sat down, grim-faced as a prisoner of war. Hillary gave him a thumbs-up but felt her gut twist as she heard McMartin's next words: "We have a Paisley Joan on the list." He looked around the room and as Paisley stood, he asked, "Last name, please?"

"Joan is my last name, sir." She strode to face the Board. "I stand as an artist before you today, a unique individual with a unique name I created myself, in the freedom we all share in this country."

The walls of the small boardroom seemed to start sliding to the right. Hillary blinked fast trying to stop them, but they picked up speed as sounds blurred together. She heard Paisley's voice as if from a far-off land. Was this her own mother testifying against her, abandoning her all over again?

Paisley's words reverberated against the four walls of the boardroom as if in an echo chamber and struck hard against Hillary's heart. "In college as in life, each person deserves to choose a pathway." A pathway, thought Hillary, that's what you call sailing away to Polynesia with your lover.

"It is wrong to force any person, be they student or artist or anyone with a dream, to pursue activity that is not a fit for them." Like you pursued your bohemian artist lifestyle.

"I say, keep that ES class but make it optional, not mandatory." Paisley sat down, this time some distance away from Hillary and did not look at her. Hillary was grateful for the distance between them, stopping her from using the jolts of energy pouring through her body driving her hands to want to slap the smug look off of her mother's face. Hillary balled her handkerchief into a knot and squeezed it as if choking her mother.

Margaret Smith clapped a be-ringed hand to her chest, as other board members' eyes widened.

"I see." McMartin fanned his face with his copy of *Robert's Rules*. "There being no more comments then, do I hear a motion regarding this issue before us?"

Margaret Smith called out in a high voice, strong as spun steel: "So Professor Zale has gone missing! Another problem related to this class! I move that to ensure peace in the community, Clearwater College immediately cancel the mandatory nature of ES 101 and allow students to choose whether to complete the course or drop it with no harm, no foul on their transcripts."

Hillary was holding her breath.

"Do I hear a second?" asked McMartin.

Justin Bierce spoke up. "As a point of discussion, Hillary Broome is not fit to teach anything here or elsewhere. The woman is a plagiarist."

Hillary felt faint. Little gasps of shock filled the room.

"However, that is a different matter, one left for closed Board sessions. For now, let's return this campus to a calm learning environment. I move to amend the motion on the floor by striking out the words 'the mandatory nature of' and add the word 'current.'"

McMartin asked him to articulate his proposal of an amended motion.

"I move that to ensure peace in the community, Clearwater College immediately cancel ES 101 and allow students to choose whether to complete the current course or drop it with no harm, no foul on their transcripts."

At the board table, gray heads were nodding in

agreement. The room filled with uh-huhs of agreement. McMartin gaveled for quiet and said, "The amended motion requires a second."

"I second the motion," called the board member seated next to Justin. A stir of voices in the room called out "Third," and Hillary saw Nettie laugh as someone yelled, "May the fourth be with us." Hillary felt the room spinning again.

McMartin pounded his gavel. "Order! Order! It has been moved and seconded to cancel the pilot project Ethnic Studies 101 class but let students in the current class choose whether or not to complete it with no harm to their transcripts. All those in favor, say aye."

The jerky humming of the AC suddenly stopped. The hot silence in the small room was peppered with the sound of "aye."

"Any nays?" asked McMartin. Not a sliver of sound could be heard.

Hillary felt a sense of vertigo, as if falling off the end of a diving board into space. She was in a foreign land, tumbling along. This is what the psychic Caty must have meant, this was killing her.

She could hear voices. Booker Williams was outlining a new proposal to Van Cleese. Claire was telling her not to be upset, that this vote would not affect her and Keisha in the Early College program.

Paisley walked over and said it was best that the class was cancelled and she was inviting the girls to the outdoor amphitheater to rehearse for the rap concert they'd been invited to perform in. They could get a ride home later from Paisley's musician friend. The three of them walked away.

Time stood still.

Dupree was tugging on Hillary's elbow. He guided her outside, telling her the girls would be okay with Paisley. "Come sit in the office, see how the search is going."

Clutching a BLM sign, Neka Jay rushed over to Hillary. "You failed us! You lost the class, now SoJust is fighting alone." Loose strands of long black hair had fallen from her bun and whipped side to side as she shook her head.

"I tried my best," said Hillary, fighting back tears. "You could have come in to the boardroom and spoken up as part of the community. Why didn't you?"

"The old white supremacy system in that boardroom is against us. I should have realized sooner that as a white woman, you don't really get it," hissed Neka Jay. "You can't really fight for us. You're even blaming us now for not commenting!"

Stunned as if she'd been punched in the face, the truth hit Hillary hard. "You are right. Find another advisor, get yourself someone of color."

Hillary ran to her SUV, jumped in and slammed the door shut. She bent her head and pressed her handkerchief onto her cheeks as if Ed's hands were there comforting her. But he was away. She had failed at everything.

A hot misery engulfed her, drowning out tears. The only one waiting at home for her was Darius, the yellow lab.

36

SAME DAY

Nettie and Frank watched a stern-faced Booker Williams leave the room through the side door to his office. Then they rushed over to Lavender Van Cleese and stood holding their fists in the air, as if they'd just won gold and silver medals. "Well done, Dean!" hooted Nettie.

Frank's smile faded as he looked in the direction of President Williams's door. "But now, Williams is going to come up with some other Critical Race Theory project, just watch."

Van Cleese nodded. "With this new Board, though, we can nip his nonsense in the bud. Let me tell you what I've been thinking."

Nettie left Frank and Van Cleese to their machinations and went outside to check on her students.

The MSNBC reporter thrust his mic in her face and asked, "How will the theft of justice for people of color be taught now that you've defeated ES 101?"

"There is no theft of justice. The past two centuries have brought us all along the path of liberty and justice through the brilliance of capitalism."

"What do you say about Hillary Broome's plagiarism?"

"What do you mean? It's an unsubstantiated charge by our new board member."

"Columbia *Spectator* carried an article on it. You never saw it?"

Nettie shook her head. "My focus is not on what others have done wrong but about what each individual can do to flourish."

She spotted her students sitting on top of tarps in the bed of the Kovar pickup and left the reporter to join them.

Barney and Lorena were standing beside the truck.

"Where's Fury?" Nettie asked.

Barney nodded in the direction of a distant stand of valley oaks. "He's having it out with Robert."

"What do you mean, having it out?"

"Fury told him he wanted a few words."

"Why?"

Barney's eyes narrowed. "Coulda been Robert spouting off mad over new orchards replacing valley oaks, their canopies bare of food and medicine after the white man killed off most of his people."

Lorena shrugged her shoulders.

Barney grinned. "Fury standing up for owning the orchard lands."

Lorena flashed Barney an evil eye.

"Okay then, Lorena might have something to say 'bout them two boys. She knows everyone's story."

Lorena smiled at Nettie and said nothing.

"Well, Barney," Nettie said, "since Fury's taken you under his wing, you let him know when he returns that I want to see him up at the big house tomorrow, twelve noon sharp."

"Yes, ma'am!" Barney nodded in his mild and likable manner.

**

Nettie marched back to the parking lot. Hormones. Even smart birds can be driven by irrational impulses. What was Fury up to?

She would have a serious talk with him. Tomorrow.

She took the back roads home, her Mercedes top down, the breeze lifting her dark hair, a cigarette holder clenched in her teeth. Tonight's victory radiated though her as she threaded the gravel roads of her orchards. This outcome would halt the campus drift toward socialism.

Nettie passed by several walnut storage sheds in the moonlight, never giving a thought to what might be going on in any one of them.

PART III

Darkness comes. In the middle of it, the future looks blank. The temptation to quit is huge. Don't. You are in good company ... You will argue with yourself that there is no way forward. But with God, nothing is impossible. He has more ropes and ladders and tunnels out of pits than you can conceive. Wait. Pray without ceasing. Hope.

—John Stephen Piper

37

THURSDAY NIGHT

Hillary sat slumped in the driver's seat of her Forester, tears on her cheeks like a salty moisturizer, her body flooded with anger. Nettie and her gang were just straight-out racists who wanted things to stay the same.

She was a fool to think she could make a difference, make this world a tiny bit better. Just like she was foolish to think Paisley would ever stand up for her. Instead, her own mother seemed to be luring her little Claire away. Same old thing. Paisley lived to fulfill her own desires.

And what would happen now that Hillary's panic that led to plagiarism so long ago had been made public?

She licked her lips, tasting the tang of her

sorrows, inhaling an ocean of regrets, swimming in self-pity. What to do? Calling Ed again wouldn't help. He was so far away. Claire had run off with Pied-Piper Paisley. Keisha's mother was dead. The class was near-dead, maybe. Worst of all in this moment, Zale was missing. She should never have run back to her office and left him alone. She had failed everyone.

Her chest barely moved with her shallow breaths, but her heart pounded like breakers crashing on sand. Sand. That was it. She would get Darius and drive to San Francisco, let him run free on Ocean Beach. She would sit on a sand dune and drown her misery. She was of no use to anyone.

Her vision still blurry, she got on 99 north, her pulse racing. As she drove past the Lodi Dojo, she realized she was missing Sensei James' class tonight. Another foolish effort. Karate wasn't any use against the assault on ES 101.

Darius was right inside her front door when she got home. "Come on, buddy, let's get away." His thick yellow tail wagged so hard it knocked over the blue ceramic butterfly on the tiered shelf by the door. She reeled back. "Oh, Darius, I know you didn't mean it."

Hillary bent to pick up the pieces. She had bought the fragile swallowtail butterfly at a benefit auction to raise money for the Ans Botha Center. The blue swallowtail spoke to her of transformation, like the one she'd had tattooed above her ankle on Claire's thirteenth birthday when she'd accepted the job of team teaching the Intro class.

And now the bird lay broken in her hand. Broken like her dream of making a difference. She went to the kitchen to throw the bright blue shards into the trash. It was all the fault of those old white people on the Board. They weren't ever going to change.

From her pantry, she grabbed a bottle of Lodi Zinfandel with a screw top, so as not to bother with a corkscrew. Then she stuck another bottle under her arm and grabbed a third one, as well. They fit perfectly into her backpack alongside a bottle of water and the collapsible bowl she always carried in the pack for Darius.

After she snapped him into his canine harness in the back seat, she took off, headed toward San Francisco. The light traffic made her sleepy, and her thoughts drifted back. She recalled last year when she drove to the City, looking to find her mother after all those years without a word from her. She remembered how Keisha hadn't heard from her mother either and the hideous reality that the woman who'd been dug up in the apple orchard was Keisha's mother.

Sometimes, Hillary wished she'd never found Paisley after all, even though she seemed like a blessing for Claire, but a mixed one for sure. Flashing red-and-blue lights lit up her rear-view mirror as a yellow Mustang flew by, a highway patrol car close behind, its siren wailing in the night. Darius howled along with it.

For distraction, she tuned in a late-night radio talk show. It featured a guest spouting his theory that depression thinned the veil between worlds. She kept the volume loud, her thoughts darting among her worlds and how she'd failed in all of them.

Hillary veered onto Highway 37, the lonely road called the Black Point cutoff. At last, she drove across the Golden Gate Bridge, thinking about people who'd given up and taken a last breath before jumping off into a salt-water oblivion. She envied them. They'd put their troubles to sleep.

The straight route south though Golden Gate Park was spooky, the night lit up by lanterns of the homeless in the park. Homeless. She felt like one of them. A loser. A failure.

She drove along parallel to the edge of the Pacific, and parked in the lot by the Dutch Windmill. Darius was eager to get out of the car, but he stood still for her to snap on his leash. She traded her pumps for the flip-flops she carried in the back of the SUV then she wedged a thin waterproof blanket into her backpack.

"Come on, boy." They climbed over some low dunes and when they got near the breakers at water's edge, she unsnapped his leash. "You're free! Go!"

He raced up and down the damp sand near the water. This was the time Hillary was grateful that Darius was different from most Labradors. He hated the water. So she didn't have to worry about him getting caught in a rip tide along this beach. Another way to let your sorrows go. But not her way.

She walked to a grassy dune, grateful for the clear sky and the full moon.

The blanket put up a struggle as she worked it out of the backpack and spread it on the sandy mound. "Let's get this party started." She opened up the collapsible bowl and poured out water for Darius.

She plopped herself down, twisted open the Lodi Zin and drank straight from the bottle. She was no longer used to a glass with dinner every evening, so the rush came quickly and edged away the hurt choking her body.

She tugged the edges of her blazer around her stomach. My big fat body, looking for justice for others. What about for me?

By the time she'd polished off half the bottle, Darius was back, shaking sand from his blond coat. He settled himself down next to her. "Good boy," she said and finished off the first bottle of Zin, tilting it high to get the last drops. She lay back on the blanket and started counting the faraway stars. What would life be like on another planet?

At dawn she woke to see an old man limping across the damp sand, working at pushing a flimsy metal cage of a cart with small wheels. It had fishing poles sticking out at odd angles like antenna on a giant crustacean.

She couldn't help staring. He looked like he was in pain, one hip sagging each time that leg stepped forward, as if he were on an invisible pier, pock-marked with holes. She sat up on the mound of beach grass, dizzy, thinking about opening another bottle of wine.

He wouldn't be going to fish into the surf would he? That would be crazy. There were fishing poles stuck into the sand, their lines taut and straight where they disappeared into the sea. But no other fishers around. Darius sat alert but didn't bother the solitary man. She opened the second bottle of Zin and hesitated. She'd never started drinking first thing in the morning before. But she was on a mission to forget about her failures. She gulped a couple swallows and sat gazing at the old man, her mind blank, before she lay back down.

She must have dozed off. Next thing she knew, the old man was coming toward her, still limping in that awful way, now pulling his cart behind him.

"Hello, there," he said.

She rubbed her face and tried to swallow, her

throat dry from the salt air. "Are you talking to me?" she croaked.

His voice was hard to hear against the crash of breakers pounding the sand of Ocean Beach. "Would you like a perch to take home for your supper?"

She sat up and pulled her blazer tight against the early morning chill as she gazed at him. He began to speak. "I had a vision, down by the river. Where it pours into the sea about a mile away." She was pretty sure there was no river there, but she nodded.

"The vision came after weeks and months and years of praying and marching and speaking out. Reading and studying the works of James Baldwin and W.E.B. Dubois. What I saw on the bank of that river was Jesus, raising his own fishing pole high up and back over his shoulder then he swiveled his body to cast into the sea. Jesus turned to me and said, 'The sharks will always be out there, but cast your line out for a meal.'"

What did the old man mean? He reached behind him into his rickety cart and handed her a fish. "Take this one home and share it."

Darius whined and pawed at the sand. Hillary reached up with both hands and accepted the cold body of the fish.

The old man said, "We feed one another." He turned and walked away without a limp.

One another. What could she do for him? She called out, "Thank you!" Without turning back, he stopped, waved and pointed to the sky. Then he carried on along the sand, parallel to the street, until he became a tiny speck and vanished.

Vanished.

Where was Zale?

38

FRIDAY, SEPTEMBER 10

How could she have run off when Zale was missing? How could she have been so selfish? *Feed one another*. Hillary tried to swallow but her throat was dry. The old man's words had warmed her chilled soul. She held the foot-long fish out, away from her wrinkled blazer. Darius sniffed at the fish.

In the fresh morning breeze, the silvery-red fish swayed as if still alive. She wasn't sure what to do with the gift of the perch. She couldn't just toss it into a waste bin. But she had to hurry and get back to hunt for Zale. Darius whined and pawed at the sand. "Come on boy, let's get home."

She wrapped the fish in the thin blanket, brushed her hands off on her pants and got Darius leashed up. She stumbled back over the beach to the sidewalk, pulled out her phone and called Dupree.

No, he said. There was no sign yet of Zale. An All-Points Bulletin was out on him. Search parties were forming.

She barely made it to the waste bin before her stomach let loose the morning's Zin.

**

At home, Claire was wide awake and waiting for her. "I was worried about you, Mom!" Claire cried. "Where did you go?"

Her daughter's piercing tones intensified Hillary's stabbing headache, a rightful consequence for having run off. "I'm sorry, but you were with your grandmother. Just had to have some space, some alone time at the beach. I've got to hurry back to school. Professor Zale is missing."

"What? Missing?" Claire stood, her mouth agape.

Hillary nodded. She rolled the perch out of the blanket and into the kitchen sink. "I have to hurry and clean this fish."

"Ugh!" Claire backed away. "Where did you get it?"

"An old fisherman gave it to me." Hillary snapped open last week's *Clarion* and whisked a few layers of newspaper into the other side of the double sink. She reached for a butter knife. "Your father and I used to camp where he went fishing as a boy. Got to hurry. They're setting up search parties, but I've got to take care of this fish."

Claire watched wide-eyed and silent as Hillary held the perch by its tail and scraped scales off the pale red-and-olive-green body onto the *Clarion*. She rinsed the fish off, and with a slim boning knife, gutted it neatly.

As she placed the cleaned fish on a layer of freezer paper, Paisley came into the room. "Impressive way to bring home the bacon." She gave out a shrill laugh. "Good image for a painting. I'll be out in the studio."

Hillary wrapped the fish and put it into the freezer, folded the newspaper around the mess, and took the bundle outside to the bin. She peeked into the studio and there was Paisley at her easel, a fish alongside a rasher of bacon already outlined in charcoal on her canvas.

Inside, Claire was finishing up her Wheaties with oat milk. She announced, "Keisha and I volunteered to help set up for unveiling a Loved Ones' Memorial Wall this weekend. Stacy said she'll drive us down to the Center." She set her empty bowl in the sink. "I'll be out in front waiting for them to pick me up."

"Go ahead," Hillary said. "Proud of you both." And it was true. They were helping build the community of compassion that was the goal of the Ans Botha Center downtown. Working on that a few years ago had been rewarding for Hillary, meeting Booker Williams on that board and getting invited to co-teach ES 101. But the class had turned into another of her failures.

Hillary took off her blazer and turned it inside out. She put in the hamper for the cleaners, washed her hands and phoned Dupree again.

While she waited for him to pick up, she held her breath, hoping they'd found Zale. Her heart sank as she heard Dupree's tired voice: "No responses yet to the BOLO. He's likely been kidnapped. He would not have wandered off."

Her stomach roiled. "What happened, exactly?"

"You and I were the last to see him, me really after you ran back to your office. I wish I hadn't gone right into the Safety Office, damn. I left him on his own to get to his car. Someone must have been watching for him."

"You had no reason to think he wouldn't make it. Don't beat yourself up."

"Could have been watching for you, as well. Ever thought about that?"

Hillary's blood turned cold in her veins. "No. No, never considered it." But there had been those comments from Lorena, one of those students living out at Nettie's.

Dupree let out a long sigh. "Okay. After you called and said he wasn't at our house, I went to the admin lot to look for him. The lot was half empty. I found his car parked and still locked. I radioed the guys directing traffic to stop cars from leaving but most had already gone. It was a hot mess. There was a Toyota parked a couple spaces down from Zale's Mazda. I saw the Toyota pull away and noticed something on the blacktop. When I got close, I could see ... " His voice choked up, "a key ring." He was silent a few beats.

Hillary recoiled at what she suspected was coming next.

"It had that little brass cross hanging on it. You know, like the one around his neck."

Hillary nodded, picturing Zale's habit of pulling out his key ring and rubbing the inch-long cross between his thumb and fingers when he was working out a problem in his mind, humming softly. "Yes," she said.

Dupree carried on. "So I radioed John at the exit to stop the Toyota. Brought the driver back for questioning. The kid was shocked to find out something had been under his car. He clearly was innocent. We suspect Zale tossed his keys there as he was being snatched, to leave us a clue."

"What about his phone?"

"Nothing. I called his number. Dead."

"How about footage from the cameras in the parking lot?"

"The camera closest to his car looks to be shot out. The alarms were so loud I couldn't hear any gunfire. The recording from the far side of the lot is hard to analyze, what with the chaos and all kinds of people running to their cars. Campus police were swamped directing traffic out of the lots. Likely the bomb threat was part of the kidnap plot. So many potential witnesses, students and staff scattered all over the place. Truth is, we're not sure where to start."

Bile rose in Hillary's stomach. The class had indeed caused this in its own way. She sighed. "There won't be another class session until next week. Even then, it's not clear if any students will show up now that it's optional. What can I do to help?"

"We've got Zale's photo up on the website as a Missing Person, labeled 'stranger abduction' and 'suspicious circumstances.' Need more media attention. We're grateful for all the help we can get in the search. You can work with your SoJust students. They're on campus. One of them came by the office and volunteered the club's services for 'boots on the ground.' I probably gave her more details than I should have." He let out a low groan.

"Okay, I'll check in with Ed and get back to you."

What was wrong with her? How could she have left while Zale was missing?

Dupree must not realize she had resigned as faculty advisor. She was going to have some serious fence mending to do. Would Neka Jay forgive her?

Her face burned with shame. Could she ever forgive herself for running off when she should have been doing all she could to find Zale?

Hillary was dripping with sweat, not sure if it was nerves or the temperature heating up or both. After a quick shower, she put on one of her chambray blouses with trumpet sleeves, perfect for the hot summers in the Central Valley. She strapped on her Apple Watch above her elbow, so much cooler than wearing it on her wrist.

Hillary called Ed. He was on his way to the airport and had just received new information. "That chain, what a freak connection but it led to a DNA match. Keisha's mother's killer is already behind bars."

Hillary gripped her phone tight to keep from dropping it. "They are sure?"

"Yes, and they've sent deputies to inform Stacy and Keisha."

Hillary was stunned. "Claire is with them on their way downtown to help set up for unveiling the Loved Ones' Memorial Wall. What a shock this will be."

"The deputies are trained to be supportive. And I'll be home this afternoon."

"Holy Mary," breathed Hillary. "There's nothing I can do for them right now. Zale is still missing. I'm going down to help search."

Then she texted Neka Jay: "Forgive me, please,

for last night. I want to help." She checked her phone every ten seconds, eager for a reply. But the young woman didn't respond. Was she angry or just caught up in the search?

Hillary decided to drive down to school. See if Neka Jay would welcome her back.

39

SAME DAY

Neka Jay stood at the front of the room. Hillary knew she owed her an in-person apology but refrained from drawing attention away from the young woman's leadership. Hillary sat near Pamela Fung at the back of the classroom. It was impressive that the Humanities professor had stepped in so quickly as faculty advisor. Now it was Hillary's turn to be a volunteer since she'd resigned as advisor, in such a rude and selfish way. She had to buck up and forget about success and perfection. She needed to just do what needed to be done.

"Hi, Pamela," said Hillary. "Glad you're here to support these eager live wires."

"After your defense of the intro class failed to convince the Board to carry it on as mandatory, I realized it will take *all* of us," said Pamela, underscoring the word *all* with air quotes, "to contribute more time, to lead the way, starting here at home on our campus."

Near the whiteboard in front, students stood at attention as if part of a military unit, looking past Neka Jay at a list printed in red marker. Hillary realized these were locations where the search for Zale was happening. Some were on campus and nearby, and others in town and along Highway 99. Dupree's phone number was at the bottom of the list.

Hillary was surprised to see a short veil covering the bun on top of Neka Jay's head. She was wearing a black T-shirt with white letters on the front spelling out SO JUST.

When Neka Jay turned to face the board, Hillary focused on the back of her shirt, which read:

SO JUST
what are
Sikh markers?

- *Kes* (hair)
- *Kanga* (comb)
- *Kara* (iron bracelet)
- *Kirpan* (small dagger)
- *Kachera* (underwear)

Hillary stared in fascination. At least one good thing had happened. The Identi-tees had arrived.

Neka Jay pointed with a short dagger at the list on the board. "Our campus law enforcement has asked for help from the FBI. They are setting up searches in these locations. We have been given the task to check out the oak groves." She tapped that line on the whiteboard with her dagger.

"Professor Zale's disappearance," she said, frowning, "is already 'high profile' because he is in immediate danger of foul play. He was last seen walking toward the admin parking lot. We'll search the meadow by the oak grove first, in an organized row, looking for anything suspicious. If you find something, take a pic and text it to Dupree at his number." She tapped the board next to his phone number three times, then tucked the knife into the back pocket of her jeans.

The students turned to each other in grim silence, broken by Bayani, who asked, "What if no one finds anything?"

Neka Jay frowned again. "If the professor isn't found soon, the FBI has his black knit kufi as a 'scent article' in a paper bag in case they need to call in a bloodhound."

Holy Mary. Hillary pictured the few times she'd seen Zale wear the short, round cap. Grim to think of a "scent article" to lead a hunt. How Darius had uncovered the crime scene at Apple Acres came to mind. A surge of sorrow washed over her.

Keisha's mother's buried body. Even though he'd not had formal canine rescue training, Darius might be useful in the search for Zale. And she could use that jacket of his, the one he'd hung on her office coat rack yesterday when the temperature soared as they worked on the WAR slides. Was that only yesterday? It seemed so long ago. The jacket could be used as a scent article. It didn't seem real to think of things like this.

"So, who's got cars?" Neka Jay was asking. "We can reimburse for gas money. The SoJust tees are already selling like snow cones on a summer day. Setting up pre-orders was a great idea, Lorena. Have you got a car?" Lorena smiled but didn't respond to Neka Jay's question. Hillary was surprised to learn that Lorena identified as a Christian from the back of her tee, anyway.

"I've got my Toyota," offered Bayani. His black tee had the same big white letters on the front as Neka Jay's, spelling out: SO JUST. But on the back his listed male Muslim markers. Hillary was amazed to see that included were trimmed pubic hair, depilated armpits and clipped nails. What all you could learn from a T-shirt!

Angel spoke up. "Shireen left our car with me today and took little Jake to work with her on the bus. Called it an adventure." Angel's belly bulged at nearly seven months along. With all the Labor Day horrors, Hillary was grateful that at least Angel hadn't lost her baby. The back of her shirt proclaimed atheist markers as Scientific Analysis; Free, open inquiry; Denial of God or gods; and Rejection of all religious belief.

Hillary raised her hand. "I can use my Forester. I'll go home and get Darius to help search." At Neka Jay's frown, Hillary added, "Labrador retrievers are good hunters."

Neka Jay laughed and retrieved the knife from her back pocket. She held it high in the air. "Welcome back, Professor Broome! You still have a role to play in this war of ours."

Hillary glowed with joy despite her hangover but noticed Lorena scowling at her.

Neka Jay asked Hillary, "How will you know where the rest of us are?"

"I'll text you when I'm back, and you can send coordinates for my GPS."

"Right. We'll be searching the meadow near the valley oaks. It's next to some private property."

40

SAME DAY

Her scalp tight in its grip of a dull headache, Hillary got back on Highway 99. She drove ten miles over the speed limit in a hurry to get to Sacramento, pick up Darius and get back to searching with the students. Keeping her focus forward, she threaded in and out of the Friday traffic.

Startled to notice her fuel level was well below a quarter tank, she took the next off-ramp, where a gas station and garage had been in business for decades, right next to her Dojo.

Fitting the nozzle into her tank, she got the pump started. It was already hot and headed for another hundred-degree day. She left the car filling on automatic and went inside the small shop that struggled to compete with the 7-Eleven a few miles away. "I'll have your 'any-size Iced Coffee' for a dollar, the largest size please." The clerk laughed as he handed her a mammoth thirty-two-ounce cup. "Bad night, huh?"

She grimaced, filled her cup halfway with ice then flooded it with super-caffeinated dark roast coffee. She took three big swigs before she raised her loose sleeve and double-checked her Apple Watch. No calls or texts had come in, so she went outside to the Ladies in the small outbuilding behind the station.

She emerged minutes later and walked along the powdery white stucco wall of the vintage station toward the front, surprised to see a Kovar Orchards pickup truck parked off to the side. What was it doing here? There was that Nettie Kovar again. Anger flared the length of her body and she reached to lift the hair off her neck.

Suddenly, something pushed at the back of her head.

"Okay, lady, your turn," a hoarse voice whispered.

Hillary gasped at a pungent smell. She slapped her hand against her forehead as a cloth was pulled over her face. At the same instant she reached her other hand up inside her sleeve to press the emergency button on her Apple Watch.

Before she could hit it, Hillary blacked out.

41

SAME DAY

Nettie opened her freezer, pulled out a plastic box of her chocolate chip cookies and set them on the counter to thaw in the sunlight. Fury would be here soon and it never hurt to sweeten up her admonitions.

She was ecstatic that ES 101 had been virtually canceled. There was still the question of how many students would want to finish out the last three weeks. She would pursue recruiting students into her expanded *You Own the Orchard* program, offer plenty of inducements. They could work toward earning their own acres of land if they chose to stay in the agriculture business.

She logged on to her computer and was thrilled to see over a hundred registrations for her orientations next week. She was going to have to shift some of her Crows from harvesting walnuts to getting the new students up and running in the program.

She glanced at the time on the computer. It was nearly twelve-thirty and no sign of Fury. It wasn't like him to ignore her. Scooting her chair back, she felt a surge of energy. She might have to take a stronger hand in dealing with Fury. Could his heroic independence and his confidence have fooled her into considering him as her smartest White Crow in recent years?

She backed her Mercedes out of the garage and stopped on the gravel road to put the top down and enjoy the sunshine. She drove the short distance to the barn dorm. As she stepped up onto the plank porch, she heard voices coming from the open kitchen window.

"Exactly." It was Lorena. Something about her loud voice made Nettie stop and listen out of sight. "Make that *bruja* think twice about blackballing me for the tutoring job. I followed her SUV and phoned her location to Fury."

"You really did that?"

"Just to scare her, you know, not hurt her, Robert."

"So where is she?"

"Fury said he would take her in the pickup and Barney could park her gas-guzzling SUV out at the shed where they are keeping Zale. Fury said he will set the two of them free soon. Let them walk out onto Highway 99 and get rescued by some, you know, people with good hearts."

"Doesn't Fury know it's a federal crime? Kidnapping?"

"He kept them blindfolded so they can't identify him. And Fury and Barney are pros at changing their voices. I'm going out to give that *bruja* a piece of my mind before the release."

"You're flirting with fire. Fury threatened me last night, made sure no one else heard him, but he showed me a place in the oak grove where he threatened to bury me if I don't keep my hands off you."

Lorena's laugh was a tinkling bell. "He doesn't mean it. He's all macho talk."

"You don't know the real Fury. I'll be here if you need me, but I don't want to get involved in this crime."

"It's no crime to be showing the world what you can and cannot tolerate." Her footsteps sounded across the floor. Nettie realized she was leaving by the door at the other side of the barn.

Nettie was appalled. Her Crows had flown way beyond reason.

Should she stop Lorena here and now? Or just go out to the storage shed and confront Fury and Barney?

42

SAME DAY

In a muggy darkness, Hillary fought to wake up. What happened? She blinked and tried to focus but could see only blackness in front of her face. Her arms were tight against her sides, her legs pressed together.

A wrapping held her encased. Something scratched against her cheeks. She began turning as if on a rotisserie.

With no warning, the sheath broke open and she teetered sideways at an edge. The word "fulcrum" hit her, just before the earth opened up.

She plunged down.

Hitting the ground hard, her senses screamed out in pain, then she lay on her back, motionless. Was she paralyzed?

She squinted in the sudden light. Beyond leafy branches above, puffy clouds hung in a pale blue sky. She stretched her hands up in front of her and wrung them, relieved to feel skin to skin. Her Mary medal dangled against her wrist. She inhaled deep, testing the cool air. Where was she?

She ran her hands along her sides and traced her fingertips in small circles over the ground, finding a surface of tiny lumps. She raised her hands near her face, rolling her thumbs against her fingers, transferring particles onto the lightweight chambray of her blouse. The smell made her think of wet grass after rain, but not quite that. She reached out to the side and scraped her nails against a damp vertical wall. Spreading her fingers into a flat palm against the earth, she knew.

This was a pit, dug into the ground. Crossing her arms in front of her chest, she felt for her Apple Watch under the chambray. She pressed the emergency button and held it a few seconds.

Would the signal reach past the dirt walls? "Holy Mary," she whispered. She rocked side to side. Her pants were still on. And her shoes, yes. She wiggled her toes. Tiny legs ran lightly across her hand. She flung the critter away.

She turned her head away from the wall. As her eyes adjusted to the dim space of the pit, she could see there was someone else there. "Hello," she whispered.

Nothing. Where was she? A sudden soft humming filled the space, a familiar hum. "Who is that? Is that you, Zale?"

She heard him clear his throat, and in a raspy voice, he began to talk. "They've got us both. We are up for the test of our lives."

Reaching out to her side, she felt the wool of his jacket. He was just a few inches from her. This was a grave dug for two.

From above, Hillary heard a woman's voice. "Why aren't the professors in the shed? What are you doing out here?"

Hillary was stunned. It sounded like that fire-ball student, Lorena. She must be near the edge of the pit. "Is that you, Lorena?" Hillary yelled. "Help us!"

A ragged growl from a different voice said, "Change in plans, sweetheart. We constructed a new home for the traitors."

As her eyes adjusted to the dim light, Hillary could make out the face of Lorena peering into the pit. "Get us help, Lorena!" she screamed.

As the young woman turned away from the edge, Hillary heard her yell, "You said you would hold the professors in the shed and let them out on the main road later. Why are they down there?"

The ragged voice got louder. "Home in the earth is better than they deserve, spreading lies to kill off white people."

"Kill off? Are you loco? They weren't trying to kill off anyone."

"Preaching critical race theory is communism, worse than murder. You know that, Lorena."

Hillary could make out Lorena's face, again looking down at her. "The only killing that witch is responsible for is the prospect of my tutoring job. Thought I wouldn't find out, ha! But you've punished her enough."

"Hanging out with that club made you soft, girl. Broome is lucky she doesn't get hanged from a tree next to Zale."

"They don't deserve to be buried alive," Lorena yelled.

"Keeps them out of sight. Skips the hanging. Gets the job done. Won't be any more trouble on campus. Rip open the bag of lime, Barney."

Hoping Lorena was not over-the-moon crazy as the others, Hillary screamed, "Lorena, call the police!

Lorena peered into the darkness of the pit. "You deserve to suffer, *bruja*! Why did you ruin my chances?"

"If you help us, you can get any job you want. You'll be a hero."

Powder began falling into the pit, dotting the dirt with white patches. Hillary pulled her chambray blouse over her head. The dust spilled onto her hands and arms, burning her skin. Zale started coughing.

"Their bodies will dissolve, leave no trace," said the man. "You should thank me, sweetheart."

"Loco! Lime preserves bodies. It does not destroy them!"

The white powder stopped falling. Hillary heard the sound of a slap.

The man growled out, "You're lucky I don't throw you in, sweetheart. Get the hell out of here!"

"I will not!"

"Barney, get her back to her car, start her engine, if she knows what's good for her."

A low voice with a southern accent spoke up. "No, sir, let's throw her on in, too. She's going to spill the beans."

Hillary heard the sounds of scuffling. Chunks of dirt from the top fell onto Hillary.

Lorena yelled, "I won't go to the police!"

"I can control her, you fool. She'll keep her mouth shut, won't you, sweetheart? Help me get her back to her car, Barney."

The voices faded away. Hillary turned to Zale. She could barely see him, it was so dark now in the pit. "Are you all right?"

"My back ... killing me," Zale muttered. She could see he was struggling to sit up, huffing and puffing and pushing against the dirt wall at his side, chunks of damp earth falling onto him. To steady himself, he pulled at a root end protruding from the soil and out with it tumbled a mass of tiny white eggs falling over both of them like a scattering of soft warm snowflakes.

Her arms burned but she was afraid to rub whatever it was deeper into her skin. "We didn't know ... what happened," she said.

"At the parking lot ... " His voice grew stronger "... two guys up against me. One had a knife ... in front of my ... face."

Hillary said nothing, waiting.

"Guy ask me, 'You see this? It's for ... cutting nuts.' He slid down my belly." Zale started coughing.

Her attention was riveted on Zale, her eyes watering from the powder. She didn't want to blink and grind in the powder.

He coughed for another minute, then was quiet a few seconds before he said, "I yelled. They said shut up if I want ... to live. I tossed my keys ... to the ground."

As Zale coughed and talked, she kept hitting the emergency button on her Apple Watch.

"They ... threw me into a truck," he said, starting to wheeze. "...knocked me out. Chloroform I guess." Zale sounded stronger, the longer he went on telling his story.

Hillary's stomach churned, reliving when she blacked out. She was amazed Zale could carry on in this situation. How were they going to get out of here?

"... rolled into a room, smelled like walnuts. One guy ... must have been on the phone. Said the tyrant's at a divine destination. Check out his church. The other guy said, 'This will support Professor Kovar's case to the Board.' Then I got kicked in the back a couple times as he said, 'Lucky for you, she's against violence. Too much of a lady I guess.'"

Oh my God, thought Hillary. It's one of Nettie's students.

"He yelled into my ear, 'But, if the Board keeps your abomination alive, I'm preparing the earth for your next lesson, said he'd show me what he's got waiting outside. I could feel rope wrapping my wrists behind my back."

Her arms burned from the powdery dust, but she knew not to try brushing it off and rub it in deeper. She pressed the Mary medal tight and the Apple Watch button, again and again.

Zale's voice grew scratchier: "He said I'd be amazed at how the new ground ripper works, better than a rototiller. After that, a door slammed shut. They left me tied up on the floor."

Hillary let out a screech as warm feet scampered across her arm. "What was that?" she cried, "Rats?"

Zale started coughing, a series of hacks. How long had he been without food or water? Hillary tightened her shoulders, compressing herself away from the grave-like pit, wondering if it would do any good to try and stand.

"I rolled to the wall and rubbed my cheek against it to get the blindfold off. I was in a storage room with a window. It was a field with lines running along it. Beyond were trees as far as my eyes could see."

Zale began humming softly, interrupted by coughing spasms.

The tune was one Hillary never heard before, a soothing and calming sound. She closed her watering eyes for a second, until something tickled the back of her neck. It skittered down into her blouse.

She struggled to stand and shook the light-weight fabric until she couldn't feel the fluttering anymore. She swept the dirt with her shoe, hoping to kill whatever that was. On tiptoes, she tried to see over the edge of the pit. It was about six inches above her five-foot eight-inch length. A six-foot grave to bury them in.

But she could see leaves, branches, trees, lots and lots of trees, She jumped up and down, focusing on the trunks. What did they look like? She jumped again and again, then, breathing hard, she sat down on the white-dusted earth.

"We're right next to an orchard," she said. "The

trunks look like that tree in your yard. Pale gray bark grafted onto a black trunk."

Zale grunted. "What I saw out the window of that shed when I got the blindfold off and stood. Walnuts."

It dawned on Hillary exactly where they were.

43

SAME DAY

Nettie pressed the Mercedes accelerator to the floor and headed to the main storage shed. Lorena must have been exaggerating. With her hot Spanish blood, the girl seemed prone to drama. Surely she was making that up about kidnapping.

Out of nowhere Lorena's white Zacua came speeding on the narrow gravel road, headed straight for Nettie's Mercedes.

Nettie honked her two-tone horn, waved and yelled, "Stop!"

The Zacua kept rushing at her. Nettie swerved onto the dirt shoulder and Lorena flew past her.

Nettie sat breathing fast at the side of the road. It took her some seconds to calm down. What was happening? Lorena should have stopped when Nettie called out to her.

The Zacua came speeding back in reverse, gravel spraying out from under the tires, and came to a dead stop. Lorena yelled out the window, "Your Crows hatched an evil plan. You've got to control them!"

The Zacua took off.

Nettie sat motionless. More drama? The truth? Nettie drove slowly to the main packing shed. Once inside, she found the usual bags of lime, rich in calcium and magnesium to increase soil fertility, stacked alongside the tools and other materials. But no one was there.

Out on the shed platform, she surveyed the panorama of her land.

Joseph would be proud of how she'd carried on. Under Fury's energetic supervision, hundreds of slender new trees stood in straight rows, next to the fallow land soon to be planted, sandwiched between the old growth walnut trees.

The John Deere tractor was parked under the shed roof overhang, at rest now after Fury had driven it all summer, turning over the soil.

There he was now, way over by the old trees, his ever-present sidekick, Barney, with him.

"Hello, Fury!" she yelled. Maybe she should have come out to check on him more often. The two of them turned and walked back to the shed. Fury held a shovel, Barney a bag of lime.

"Hey, Professor, that new farm ripper is way

better than what I used last year." Fury smiled his crooked grin. "Your trusty John Deere hauled those new steel shanks along like cutting through butter. Ripped right through the hardpan and broke it up quick and way deeper than last summer."

Nettie brushed her bangs across her forehead and nodded.

"We are prepping the fallow soil for your Free Acres competition." He planted his feet and slammed his shovel a half inch into the clay soil.

She pointed at the bag Barney was carrying. "What are the shovels and lime for? What's going on?"

"Well, Professor, we know you are against violence," Fury said, stabbing his shovel at the hardpan, "but I had my ways to help you get that class shut down, you know, make sure it's really gone."

Nettie narrowed her eyes. "It was canceled on the merits of the case I argued. No need for violence."

Fury laughed. "What do you think was the turning point?"

"What do you mean? The Board followed my reasoning."

Fury rolled his eyes. "What about the impact of that bomb threat yesterday morning?"

Nettie stared at him, her eyebrows furrowed. She wiped the back of her hand across her forehead, drawing her dark bangs off to the side again. "What do you mean?"

Fury let out a guttural guffaw. "Who do you think snatched up Professor Zale?"

Nettie whispered, "You?"

Fury stabbed his shovel into the dirt, yanked it around and forced out a wedge of clay. "Then the urge came over me." A glassy sheen slipped over his eyes. "I felt strong, hauling his big black body out of the truck." He took a step closer to Barney. "My buddy here got his juices going then, too. He's from the South, you know?" He laughed and punched Barney lightly on the chin.

Nettie's heart was pumping fast. She was stunned. How had she never seen this side of him? Or had she just ignored the early warning signs, too eager to idolize him as a Howard Roark of California agriculture and make her proud. This was no time to figure it out. She had to get out of here. "So, all right, the class was cancelled. Where is Professor Zale?"

"By late evening last night when we learned the demon class was canceled, couldn't stand to just let that nigger go free, had him tied up so long lying on the shed floor, held down. A hankering came over me to lift him up, hang him from one of those big trees out there." Fury's eyes bulged and he turned to look at the stand of old walnut trees.

"It all came back to me, what my father did to them niggers trying to horn in on the Mexicans picking crops. Father couldn't let that happen. Had to scare 'em off, you know. Hang 'em in the very place they wanted to work, send a message. He let me help him. Later we buried 'em, keep it quiet from the law."

Fury stared right through Nettie, his lips clamped, his brows forming a deep V, his chest heaving. His fists worked their way up and down the shovel handle as if he were climbing a rope. "Then Barney and I had our first fight."

Nettie was at a loss for words, facing the two men in a triangle of silence.

Barney cleared his throat and spoke up. "Couldn't hang him from a tree, out in the open when students are coming to check out your Who Owns the Orchard, ma'am. Told Fury we could easy dig out from between ripper slots, wait 'til morning light, make us a pit, throw him in there. Not kill him, give him a chance to dig his way out."

Fury nodded. "Barney had something there, he did."

The horror washed over Nettie. "Where is Professor Zale now?"

Fury and Barney looked over at the old walnut tree nearest the shed but didn't say a word.

Nettie pulled her phone from her pocket, attempting to call 911, but Fury snatched it from her hands. "Can't let you do that, Professor."

She still strained for it, but he held it away from

her easily, slipping it into his shirt pocket. Then, he grabbed her arms, whipping them behind her back. She cried out in pain.

"Get the rope," he said to Barney.

Nettie twisted and broke lose, yelling, "I cannot believe you are doing this, Fury. It's so beyond the scope of reason."

Barney grabbed her, as she screamed, "You can't do this!" Fury tied her wrists together. They laid her on the shed platform and tied her ankles together, a gag in her mouth.

Fury pulled her phone from his pocket and made a call. He pinched his nostrils and shouted into the phone, "Your man Zale is in PriceCuts superstore, look in the men's apparel section."

He placed Nettie's phone on the platform and picked up his shovel. With the flat blade of the shovel, he smashed the phone until it was broken to pieces. He scooped them up and handed them to Barney. "Let's go tell Professor Zale how his colleague tried to save him."

Dazed and lying prone on the shed platform her Joseph built so long ago, Nettie watched the two of them stride away, Fury with a shovel in hand, Barney with a bag of lime, toward Joseph's old walnut orchard.

44

SAME DAY

Hillary tried to ignore the itching, burning layers on her skin. Zale was humming softly but had stopped talking. "Are you okay?" she asked.

He coughed. "Mmmm. Praying ... " His voice faded away.

"Zale?" She reached out her hand. There he was, not six inches away. Hillary felt her heart skip a beat. "Let's keep talking."

"Mmmm."

"Okay, so then, what happened? How did you get down here?"

"Just past dawn, I heard the guys come in. Barney said, 'You were right, it was quick work to dig a grave, later we can dust him with lime and be done with it. Now let's get a tarp from the pickup.'"

Hillary blinked back tears. They meant nothing in the face of such horror.

"I was hoping they'd give me some water but didn't want their attention, so I played possum. Later, they came back and got the shovels out again. Fury was excited and talking about a call he got from Lorena. She was wanting to kidnap you, too, Hillary."

Hillary froze. She was part of a plot.

"I heard Fury tell Barney to dig out enough room for two, get rid of the class and the traitor teachers, too. He seemed happy to get on the good side of Lorena."

Hillary's eyes followed the walnut leaves dancing high above her as Zale talked. She held up her arms to the light and was nearly mesmerized by the leafy shadows on her skin as she listened to Zale, so close by her side in the pit.

"They untied me. I was too weak to fight them. I asked for water but they laughed and rolled me up in a tarp, hooting they were making a hot dog on a stick."

Hillary felt like throwing up.

"With me inside they pulled the tarp over a threshold and pushed it off an edge. I fell about a foot down and then they pulled the tarp over the ground."

Hillary stretched to wrap her arms around her knees and rocked in a fetal position. She could feel the Apple Watch above her elbow but it was not bringing any help. There was nothing she could do. Nothing. Just like there was nothing she could do about racism. Nothing she could do to fix the problem. She wanted so much to be one of the saviors, but look at how that turned out.

"I'm sorry," she murmured. "This is the land of the shadows, what I wanted to help save people from."

"The shadow gives a cool space to reflect in," said Zale. "A place to own what has been stolen."

Ownership, though Hillary. A blessing or a curse? She nodded her head as she rocked.

Zale carried on, his voice urgent. "You can still help. This will never be heaven. This is earth. This culture scorns powerlessness, lamentation, and any form of failure."

"Failure. Like I wouldn't admit mine," she whispered, shame heating the powder on her arms even hotter.

"It's no wonder you have not learned to carry your shadow side, it's not shouldered by most of the schools or the church. But it can be a good teacher, the land of the shadow," Zale said, his voice growing weaker. He paused a few seconds, then continued. "The shadow is not to be avoided, denied, fled, or explained away. Like Ezekiel the prophet, we must eat the scroll that is 'lamentation, wailing, and moaning.'"

The lime powder ate away at Hillary's skin. It burned and branded her as worthless. Abandoned.

She remembered keeping her mother's absence a secret. Never inviting friends home after school. The house noiseless. Hiding under her bed in a thunderstorm, praying for Daddy to get home from the newsroom. Imagining her Camp Fire Leader as her mother during that quick hour of meeting each week. Saying she was busy and couldn't go to birthday parties because she had no mother to throw a party for her.

In high school, working on the school paper, explaining that her mother had died in a car wreck, grateful for the father she had, teaching her the ropes of being a reporter, covering the state capitol news.

Zale was talking. In the dim light of the pit, Hillary stared at Zale. What more must he have suffered than she? So much more.

Hillary felt a worm crawl across her arm. She let it be. Killing it would do no good. Her karate would not do her any good this time. She could not fix this. This must have been what that psychic, Caty, was talking about.

Hard bits of something were falling on her head. The voice with the southern accent yelled, "Here's a phone for you to call for help. Professor Kovar sent it with her regards."

Pain swelled inside Hillary's lips and spread

itself onto her cheeks and jaw. She pushed her Apple Emergency button. But nothing happened except a downpour of white powder. She couldn't stop herself from screaming, "No, no, no!"

Was this really going to cost her her life?

45

SAME DAY

Nettie's spirits lifted at the sounds of crunching along the gravel road. She wriggled around to watch the Zacua pull in and park next to her Mercedes. Lorena jumped out of the driver's side, ran to the Zacua's trunk, and pulled out a bundle of rope with flat boards attached. She held it out in front of herself.

Nettie was surprised to see who got out of the passenger side. It was Robert, a pistol in one hand. With the other, he took the bundle from Lorena.

"Where is this pit?" he asked.

"There's Professor Kovar," shrieked Lorena, pointing at Nettie. "Help me get her untied."

The two of them made quick work of freeing Nettie, and without bothering to rub her sore wrists, she jumped off the platform. She sprinted ahead, across the plowed land of her orchard towards the sounds of screaming coming from the edge of the trees.

Fury and Barney each stood by a half-full bag of lime propped against a mound of dirt, shoveling powder into a pit in the ground.

"Stop!" yelled Nettie.

Fury pivoted to face Nettie and Lorna, shouting at Robert, "Bow and arrow to the rescue, Tonto?"

Robert ran to the edge of the opening. He threw down the bundle of rope ladder while keeping one arm clutched around its end. With his other hand, he aimed his pistol at Fury.

Fury lifted his shovel, thrust it forward and swung at Robert.

Robert fired and pivoted away.

Fury's shovel hit the bare ground. He clutched his stomach and teetered, then fell into the pit.

**

Fury fell, face up, on top of Hillary. She gasped, the breath knocked out of her. He moaned and rocked back and forth.

"Grab the ladder," Zale yelled.

"What ladder?" Hillary couldn't see anything, her eyes in a pool of tears she dared not wipe away.

"Feel for it. I can see it. It's just above you."

"He's on me. I can't move."

"Hang on." Zale grunted twice more, and Fury's body rolled to wedge between them. Zale wheezed, then yelled, "That rope with the board. Stand up and climb out on it."

Half-blind, Hillary sat and leaned against the dirt wall to steady herself. She folded one leg under the other and stood, reaching up to feel for a board. There it was, jiggling against the crumbly wall of the pit. She looked down toward Zale but could only make out the dark mass of Fury's body covering Zale from her view.

"Go on," Zale yelled. "Get out."

She clutched the ropes stretched tight between two boards. Raising her arms high, she held on and lifted her foot.

The board felt firm beneath her shoe, still on her foot after all this. She straightened and let her body sway a bit as she steadied herself. She put her other foot on to the next board. Her thighs tightened. This was going to work.

Near the top, she took one more step. Flinging herself forward, she collapsed onto the ground.

Hands latched onto her and pulled her away from the edge. She could hear voices. "Get down there and help! I've called 911."

46

SAME DAY, EVENING

Hillary felt for her wedding band. Where was it? She opened her eyes as she raised her left hand, tethered by an IV line taped onto it. Her arms were bandaged. Her heart raced. She touched her face to feel gauze covering her skin all the way to her earlobes.

A beeping sounded nearby. A pale blue curtain encircled her. She lay in a hospital bed. A pattern of navy-blue dots on the curtain held her attention for a moment, until she cried out, "Help!"

The curtain flew back, and Ed bent to whisper in her ear. "You're okay, Genevieve. Everything's going to be all right."

"Where's … " She rolled her lips, loosening the gauze near her mouth. "Zale?"

"He's in the next cubicle, getting treatment." Ed brushed her hair back off her temple and nuzzled her ear. "Dupree's with him. You were both given light sedation, then the lime was removed from your skin and they applied ointment to the affected areas."

She held up her gauze-wrapped arms. He nodded. "The bandages are to keep the ointment undisturbed for twenty-four hours."

Suddenly a masked nurse in pink scrubs was at her side. "Just try to relax. The doctor will be in soon." The nurse's lanyard tag showed Hillary she was in a Lodi hospital.

Hillary nodded. Her heart rate slowed, and she dozed off. A few minutes later, she came to. She pictured the last thing she remembered, being pulled across the ground of Nettie's walnut orchard.

She twisted her head slowly from side to side on the pillow, testing her stiff neck muscles. Ed was seated next to her bed. "What happened? she asked him.

"You're safe, Zale's safe." Ed assured her. "That's enough for now," he said.

"No." She pushed herself up on her elbows to half sitting. "No, I'm fine. How did that ladder get into the pit?"

"It was the damnedest thing. That student of Nettie's, Robert Eaglefeather, he threw it in. Fury swung at him with the shovel and Robert shot Fury, in self-defense."

Hillary lay still, her mind working out the scene and suddenly she remembered Neka Jay. "Any word from the SoJust students?"

"They were at the edge of the orchard, in the old oak groves. Came running when they heard the gunshot." He held up a clear plastic bag with her things in it. "This Apple Watch of yours, signal never made it out of the pit."

Hillary stared at her husband and tried to piece it all together. "Where's Fury?"

"The kid didn't make it. Shot in the belly, bled out in the ambulance."

Hillary raised one hand and raked her fingertips through her hair. "Bled out?"

"He's gone," said Ed. "Gone."

Hillary sat up and threw her legs over the side of the bed. "What about telling Keisha about her mother?"

"I just came from downtown, went to that Memorial Wall with the deputy to inform Keisha and Stacy. At first, they grabbed each other and stood rocking and moaning, but then they crumbled to a bench and stared up at Claire and me. We stayed with them while they talked about what to do next."

Hillary's eyes filled with tears. She shook her

head slowly and reached out for the big white hand-kerchief Ed was handing her.

"I want to go check on Zale."

"You need to wait for the doctor, Genevieve."

Hillary smiled. He had changed his nickname for her. One tiny success. So many to go.

47

THURSDAY, SEPTEMBER 16

Out in front of the auditorium, Hillary noticed the students lined up at the SoJust Identi-tees table. Neka Jay's supervision of the robust fundraiser underscored her bright future as a social justice activist.

As Hillary walked inside, she reflected on the tragedy that Coach Hutcheon's life was cut short, and he missed seeing these students flourish. And he missed growing older with his wife and his twin grandbabies, who would never get to know him. Hillary felt confident the Board would approve re-naming the gym as the Hutcheon Recreation and Wellness Center.

A few days ago, Hillary and Zale had agreed to shift to a new manner of presenting today's class. They were calling it "A White Shadow Week."

It was to be a panel discussion of the events that took place between Labor Day and Friday of last week. Zale was still suffering significant respiratory effects from his ordeal and Hillary was covered with a rash. She was surprised that Nettie had not been held for questioning longer, considering her culpability in the series of hate crimes. Still, Hillary was grateful at what seemed to be her new attitude and willingness to participate on the stage with them. Lorena and Robert had agreed to participate as well, and the SoJust faculty advisor, Pamela Fung, had volunteered to be moderator.

No one knew how many students would attend, given that the class was now optional. Dean Van Cleese and Frank Stern were adamant in their opposition to what they considered showcasing the violence so close to home. They made it clear they would not attend.

President Williams texted Hillary that he planned to sit in the auditorium and take notes. As the panel members took their seats on stage, Hillary was thrilled to see the auditorium about half-full.

The house lights dimmed, and Pamela began speaking. "As the new faculty advisor for the Social Justice student club, dedicated to diversity, equity and inclusion at Clearwater College, I welcome you. Today's class session is a look beneath the surface of the deadly shadows we have witnessed and experienced recently," Pamela said. "It is an account of how some people experienced the ideas and actions of one student who lost his life in horrific circumstances proceeding from his own shadow."

Slides of the Labor Day speakers, one after another, were projected onto the huge screen behind the panel. "On Labor Day Monday, freedom of various kinds was on display in the town park," she said.

The slides changed to videos of the burning flag and the burning coffin poster in the park.

Then a slide of a social media page appeared, showing a photo of a howling baby, with a long caption above the picture:

A second slide followed showing a vast acreage of fully-leafed-out trees.

The screen turned to black. The house lights came on. Lorena began speaking. "I was attracted by Fury's story of his Army mentor, a Hispanic officer whose background was not that different from his. When Fury got out of the Army, he wanted to own orchards and hire Mexicans, to elevate them out of oppression by white ranchers." She shook her head slowly and pulled on her long black braid. "But I could never tell if he was against me or for me—me and my people."

It struck Hillary that she wasn't sure whether Lorena was for or against the aims of the club or the class. A real shape-shifter, she was. Hillary had learned how much more complicated becoming an ally of people of color was than she'd first thought.

She still had so far to go, so much to learn, so much to do.

She studied the faces of the students in the audience, their jaws slack, their pens lying flat on their handouts. Some were the ones who knew and others were just waking up. The work was daunting.

Nettie took the mic and said, "When Fury came to me a little over a year ago, he was a handsome blue-eyed man, a hero type. He told me he yearned to be a landowner like my late husband Joseph and asked to work at my ranch while he took classes in Agricultural Management.

"I accepted him into my Entrepreneurial program as a supervisor for my White Crows, as Joseph named them, for being rare and special. Willing to be individuals, different from the common herd. Fury was a go-getter of the first order, reading my books and in sync with the rhetoric of John Galt and Howard Roark. At the time I was thrilled. But now, I am shocked that I never saw what was going on under Fury's surface. But he did." She handed the mic to Robert.

Robert stood and glared at Nettie. "I overheard Fury rant about hunting union workers, professors, Black and indigenous people and other ethnic populations, even though he said he loved Hispanics and considered them white due to their Spanish heritage."

The screen lit up again with another of Fury's

social media pages, showing a giant page from the Clearwater Catalog, where ES 101 had been added. Over those typed words was printed in red:

"My blood is boiling forcing students into this race traitors class. Got to protest, "snowball" Orientation Day, hang dolls near gym, hand out Freedom Manifestos, hook up with Righteous Order, save our white people."

**

The screen went black. Lorena reached for the mic. "I will work community service for my part in the kidnapping. But when I saw how far gone Fury was in his hatred, I called 911." She looked down the table at Hillary and Zale. "I had no idea he would take it that far and I'm grateful Robert could come to the rescue." She handed the mic to Nettie.

In a trembling voice, Nettie told the rest of the story. "After Robert shot Fury, Barney surrendered to officers who arrived. Fury died at the hospital. I found Fury's story on his social media page but I was too late. He wanted his father's love and respect but his father has been locked up for years in San Quentin. We have now learned that Chuck Underwood killed in the manner of Juan Corona and buried bodies in all kinds of orchards, up and down the state. Even in my neighbor's orchard where the remains of a woman named Tamika were just discovered a few weeks ago."

Learning that Fury's father murdered Tamika had sickened Hillary at the same time it brought a horrible closure to the mystery for Stacy and Keisha. The line from the Pink Triangle Park in San Francisco came to Hillary. About the individual and the community. Where was the right balance? She stood and waved her hand at Nettie. "You intended to promote the individual and you did: you lifted Fury to the pinnacle of his selfish fantasy."

Nettie nodded and said, "My Joseph was not an extremist. He and I believed in free enterprise, but never with the use of violence. This tragedy has convinced me of my responsibility for the well-being of my White Crows community, which some even call a collective. I am in process to modify my adherence to the benefits of rational capitalism and stark individualism. There can be a middle ground."

Zale cleared his throat and in his hoarse voice said, "While independence has its worth, it cannot trump justice in the long run, and both of them are at the mercy of freedom."

Hillary stood and said, "Thank you for coming to this abbreviated class session. Professor Zale and I had a grand vision for Introduction to Ethnic Studies. It was to build collaboration among students and staff, to create a space for telling the truth in order to break out of isolation and ignorance that holds oppression in place." Her heart pounded against that hot iron ball she carried inside, the uneven mix of desire and sorrow.

"In the beginning, I thought everyone should be taught to think of community as the goal in ES 101, but I understand how some can think first of the I, the individual. I now believe making ethnic studies optional can support people to make a conscious choice, in the context of community, make a move to the middle as a form of resistance in an unjust world. Thank you to those of you who have shown up today for choosing to stay with us. We will carry on next week. The homework is to reflect on what you have experienced and to write about what you want to learn to do next."

Backstage with Zale, Hillary was nearly in tears. "This went as well as it could, the both of us barely able to carry on."

Zale nodded. "The light is slow to dawn but it is on the horizon."

She sighed. "Yes, but I'm glad plagiarism was not mentioned today. I know I should get over dwelling on it. But you can see, it's got me stuck every time I think I'm free."

His serene face a mirror of the Buddha, Zale nodded and said, "Consider a controversial claim I never forgot from *Theology Today*. It was by a preacher who said, "All wisdom is plagiarism; only stupidity is original."

She held the quote to her heart like a paradoxical balm, a gift from Grover Zale. Plagiarism during panic attacks when assigned to write stories about bad mothers in the years she was a reporter had been Hillary's hidden shame for so long. And she still had such a rocky relationship with her own mother.

Now, though, the plagiarism was not a secret anymore but a conundrum to puzzle out with others in a deeper way. President Williams had asked her to offer workshops on the topic. The man was always holding open the door of challenge.

But more important was that Intro to Ethnic Studies would continue, and would point to action built on knowledge rather than simply good-hearted intention alone. People would have to choose to take the class, true enough. So part of her job now meant getting out and selling the value of it instead of students being forced to take it.

She was ready for this new part of the work.

48

SUNDAY, SEPTEMBER 19

On this hundred-degree Sunday afternoon, Hillary's sun hat shielded her face and a loose-sleeved chambray blouse covered her arms. She walked through Cesar Chavez Park toward the Ans Botha Center, between Ed and Claire, toward the unveiling of the city's first Memory Wall.

Ahead of them and setting a brisk pace were Stacy and Keisha, arms linked, purple scarves tied around their wrists, steadfast in their support of bringing back the Monarchs, WNBA basketball to Sacramento.

Paisley had said she didn't believe in communal art projects, that they were antithetical to the independent spirit of the artist. Claire had begged her to come along, in honor of murdered victims of hatred toward gays and people of color. But Paisley could not be budged.

Hillary fingered the Mary medal hanging on her black bead bracelet. Forgiveness. What Mary's son had taught. Father forgive them, they know not what they do. Surely her mother had not known what she had done. And was still doing, so bonded to her vision of the independent artist's way.

How could Hillary truly forgive her? With a heavy heart, she tucked the problem into the back of her mind, where it had lain in wait so many decades.

As her group neared the intersection, they slowed to join with dozens of people, converging for the unveiling ceremony on the broad grassy side of the Ans Botha Community Center. Its west wall was draped with rose-colored bunting. TV camera crews and reporters stood at the ready.

Sacramento's mayor stood at the side and addressed the crowd. "Welcome all of you on this historic day at the Ans Botha Center, named for the 75-year-old Olympic coach in South Africa, the great-grandmother who passed on her wisdom to the next generation, showing that people of every race can excel at every age and place. Coincidentally, today is Grandparents' Day, a fitting time to honor families in our community, and especially those who mourn the loss of loved ones whose lives were stolen by violence. These people will never be forgotten, neither their faces nor their names, thanks to this, the first one of our 'REMEMBER US' projects."

He waved his arm across the breadth of the west wall of the Center. The bunting fell to the ground and a sunlit-washed mural of ten faces shone over the crowd, silent for long seconds.

In turns, family and friends of each person took the mic and spoke about what their lives had meant and how they would live on in memory. Hillary stood, misty-eyed and moved to see Stacy and Keisha's faces rapt with enthusiasm, nodding along as they took in each of the stories.

Later, after they'd placed their orders in a nearby restaurant, Stacy said she had an announcement. "We're proposing Tamika to be on the next REMEMBER US mural." She nudged Keisha who was sitting beside her.

Keisha nodded, a fierce look on her face. "It's planned to be in the Oak Park Community Center, right near where my mother grew up. And I did, too." She stretched her arm around Stacy's shoulder. "Love you, my grandma, who raised me up."

Claire beamed as if she herself had completed a winning play in a basketball game, and Ed raised his glass of ale. "Here's to Tamika, may she Rest In Peace."

Hillary's throat tightened. It was all about

family, about community, about learning how to stop so many kinds of violence. She would keep up her small part in the battle against ignorance and hatred that was like a curse, calling for everyone's commitment to change.

THE END

AFTERWORD

SOCIAL JUSTICE CRIME FICTION, A NEW SUB-GENRE

The 2017 psychological film "Get Out" set the tone for *Social Justice Crime Fiction*. Canadian novelist Sheena Kamal writes that this sort of film and fiction examine "a particular social issue and try to serve justice in some kind of way—or at least attempt to deepen the reader's understanding of that issue."

The Hillary Broome Novels are usually categorized as crime fiction—some are rather graphic horror stories while others are subtle family drama, and still others are travel adventures. But they did not fit neatly into a traditional fiction sub-genre such as romance, fantasy, cozy—or even traditional mystery.

To paraphrase one reader: Gillam's books are a bit hard to classify. *House of Hoops* isn't a sports story, although basketball plays an important part.

There is crime but no mystery, and there is adventure but no wild chase scenes. Social issues and family problems touch the characters' lives, but they aren't fully the focus, either. The books are simply good stories about interesting people in challenging situations.

Good stories about interesting people in challenging situations. Yes, but not a precise fit into a sub-genre category. Until the arrival of Social Justice Crime Fiction.

A piece in Bookriot.com by Emily Martin notes that Social Thriller novels, virtual twins to Social Justice Crime Novels, use "elements of suspense, horror, and mystery genres to explore and point out issues of oppression and societal inequities ... A good social thriller will make you think and have you reexamining the world from a fresh perspective."

I hope readers of Hillary Broome Social Justice Crime Novels are both entertained and informed from fresh perspectives.

June Gillam
November 2022

ACKNOWLEDGMENTS

I've been inspired by other writers who have illuminated issues around racial justice such as Debby Irving, Jodi Picoult and Christine Sleeter; by programs like the UNtraining: Healing personal & social oppressions and Becoming Beloved Community; and by my San Joaquin Delta College colleagues' energy and vision to educate ourselves and our students toward the goal of leveling the playing field for all people.

Nest of White Crows was built on four branches of my personal tree of knowledge:

- My family's experiences in working to understand our racism
- California's AB 1460 law compelling Cal State University students to pass an ethnic studies class before graduating with a bachelor's degree
- Past, present and future opposition to AB1460's mandate from various forces and stakeholders

- My work co-creating educational programs supporting equity in the California Community Colleges, with raised sensitivity to social justice issues and the relationships among white people and people of color

I knew this book would not be a metaphorical "house" like the first four books in the series, but would instead be a "nest," in which my readers and myself could observe a place that might shelter the rare, individual and attention-getting white crow.

The color "white" is used in the title in an ironic sense. In Western cultures, it often conveys a sense of purity, cleanliness, and peacefulness. In many Eastern cultures, however, white is linked to death and sadness.

What is a white crow? It is a bird exactly like a black crow, but completely white—not an albino, doesn't have the pink eyes—but with inability to produce melanin, so its feathers grow in white.

On *Whats-Your-Sign.com*, Avia claims that white crows signify unveiling secrets where "New ideas are sparked, new thought patterns are created, and a renewed intelligence forms within us that helps us find solutions to problems and **clear out old mental blocks** we struggled with in the past."

Reaching for new emotional and mental intelligence is what I've attempted in Nest of White

Crows. I'd love to hear back from you on what you got from the book.

—June Gillam, PhD.

KEY WEBSITES

Debby Irving: Racial Justice Educator and Writer.

www.debbyirving.com

Jodi Picoult. www.jodipicoult.com

Christine Sleeter: Author. Speaker. Teacher. Activist.

www.christinesleeter.org

The Untraining: Healing Personal & Social Oppressions

https://untraining.org

Becoming Beloved Community

https://www.episcopalchurch.org/beloved-community/

History of Delta College Cultural Awareness Program https://www.deltacollege.edu/student-life/cultural-awareness-program/history-cultural-awareness-program

Resmaa Menakem: Embodied Anti-Racist Education

https://www.resmaa.com

NEXT

ABOUT THE AUTHOR

June Gillam writes the Hillary Broome crime novel series, inspired by her obsession with what makes ordinary people mad enough to kill. A native of the Central Valley, June lives cradled between California's Coastal Range and the Sierra Nevada mountains. She loves the company of writers and readers and was honored with a Jack London Award for her service to the writing community. June's work is published through her imprint, Gorilla Girl Ink. Visit her at www.junegillam.com

Nest of White Crows is book five in the social justice crime novel series.

Grab your free copy of House of Hoops at junegillam.com or here:

HOUSE OF CUTS

When bodies of retail managers turn up as superstore displays in the Central Valley, reporter Hillary Broome's articles catapult her byline into the national spotlight— and she's terrified the attention could expose her shameful secrets. Working with detective Ed Kiffin, Hillary races to find the killer after he kidnaps the woman who's become the mom Hillary's always wished for.

"House of Cuts builds towards a powerful climax, reminiscent of Silence of the Lambs."

—Susan Rushton

HOUSE OF DADS

After Hillary Broome's cousin Ted collapses during a funeral, she discovers a network of jealousy, greed and secrets destroying families. Hillary already has her hands full trying to decide whether to elope with detective Ed Kiffin. Now, she's forced to investigate deadly black mold spreading through a housing development and stop a murder-in-progress that puts her own life in danger.

"Memorable characters and authentic setting make this a book you'll want to add to your must read list!"

—R. Franklin James

HOUSE OF EIRE

Hillary Broome, journalist-turned-ghostwriter from Lodi, California, and her detective husband Ed Kiffin fly to Ireland for a postponed honeymoon, expecting a romantic romp and genealogical outings. But digging into Hillary's Irish roots entangles them in a theme park developers' deadly conspiracies. It's not the holiday they hoped for in the land of a thousand welcomes.

"An exciting thriller with outstanding character development, perfect pacing and a lot of Irish historical details and cultural trivia presented naturally through the plot."

—María Andrea

HOUSE OF HOOPS

Mass shootings. Protest marches. Local government corruption. Hillary Broome's Sacramento community is facing unprecedented suffering, yet she's optimistic that a soon-to-open community center downtown will raise spirits. When Hillary becomes the target of a bitter college professor fighting urbanization, she threatens to reveal his past crime. Before she can, her basketball phenom daughter is hit by setbacks that force Hillary to confront memories of her own mother and the abandonment Hillary has been unwilling to forgive.

"In her timely novel, Gillam pits Hillary against a villain who plays by his own rules to preserve a way of life he's obsessed by. Thought-provoking and filled with suspense!"

—Linda Townsdin

NEXT

~COMING SOON~

Fallen Kings

by June Gillam

I remember when I would help Father Joseph out in the vineyard, tying the trailing grape vines to the long wires along the fence tops. It was hot and sweaty work but he promised me that we would go into the village after the week's work in the monastery was complete.

I loved the village where I could watch all the beautiful women, feeling the vegetables in the market bins and calling out how overpriced the eggplant was or the persimmons. Especially the cuts of beef for bistekka—they would try and get the butchers to slice it thinner. Just for me, one would say, batting her long black eyelashes. Another would shake her shoulders so her white cotton blouse gathered at the neckline would shimmy back and forth while she asked for a better price on the meat.

Father Joseph always hurried me away from the vendors where the women liked to haggle with the butchers. He took me to the bookstore and set me on a stool to look through The Malleus Maleficarum, warning me to stay away from women who were practicing witchcraft. I could hear him over in the corner talking to the bookstore owner in a soft voice, his dark eyebrows pulling down his bald scalp as he frowned.

Father Joseph was in charge of me at the crumbling old monastery. The other orphans had been sent away to a different place—I don't know where. I remember now that at first I felt special getting to stay with Father Joseph in the big old stone building. It was crowded then, with many men out helping in the vineyard. They wore brown robes with white ropes around their waists. They called each other "brother." I used to call the other orphans brother too, before they started laughing at me and sneaking up behind me in the rows of grapes and punching me in the shoulders and calling me pigface.

Father Joseph would call me indoors then, and let me read his lives of the Saints books. I remember how sad he was when the brothers got sent away to a different place, and took all the other orphans along with them. But I was glad.

I'm still glad to be here, all grown up, in this big old stone building, with some men who feel like real brothers to me. In a different kind of a way.

Nest of White Crows is book five in the social justice crime novel series. Fallen Kings will be book six.

Grab your free copy of House of Hoops at junegillam.com or here: